HEATED RIDE

Hellions Motorcycle Club

CHELSEA CAMARON

D1519618

HEATED RIDE

The Hellions Ride

HELLRAISERS DEMANDING EXTREME CHAOS

USA TODAY BESTSELLING AUTHOR

Chelsea Camaron

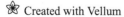 Created with Vellum

INTRODUCTION

Heated Ride

Marriage is a commitment for life ... so is patching in to the Hellions motorcycle club.

Jenna "Vida" Natera de Castillo has given her life to being Ruby's ol' lady and a mother to their three children. She takes her commitment to him seriously.

Ruben "Ruby" Castillo has lived a life of hard-knocks. Working day in and day out to make his situation better, he's focused.

People change and passion can fizzle over time.

Life for Jenna falls apart the day Ruby no longer says "I do" to the life they have built.

Keeping the fires burning in a marriage is hard. Will the chaos of the club bring them back together, or is it what pulls them further apart? Will these two find the flame again? **Will their love find a new spark on their heated ride through life?**

Series Reading Order:

Inner list:

One Ride

Forever Ride

Merciless Ride

Eternal Ride

Innocent Ride

Simple Ride

Heated Ride

Ride with Me (Hellions MC and Ravage MC Duel) co-written with Ryan Michele

Originals Ride

Final Ride

DEDICATION

DEDICATION

To my hubbub. This year, we celebrate fourteen years of marriage. The day we said I do was the day I married my very best friend for the good, the bad, and the ugly. We have seen hard times, and we have worked through them side by side. Ride or die, baby, till my very last breath and beyond, you're stuck with me. Always remember, "I'm not signing shit." I love you in the now, for the past, and for the future.

To Jenn, ride or die, you've been a Hellions ol' lady since before *One Ride* released. Thank you for always having my back, all of your input, and reading every book time and time again until we get it just right. I love you to pieces and couldn't imagine this journey without you.

To anyone who has fought to make their marriage survive, this book is for you. It's not always easy to stand by the person who has the power to hurt you beyond repair. It's not easy to keep the home fires burning when it all seems to be going up in smoke right in front of your face.

CONTENT WARNING

This book contains mature content not suitable for those under the age of 18. Content involves strong language and sexual situations. All parties portrayed in sexual situations are over the age of 18. All characters are fictional.

This book is not meant to be an exact depiction of a motorcycle club but rather a work of fiction meant to entertain.

LETTER TO THE READER

Dear Reader,

This entire series is a very personal one for me. This particular book takes me back to a time in my life when my own marriage was on the brink of divorce, and I had to learn to stand on my own. In the process, I learned that, in being married and having children, I had lost myself. In finding myself again, my husband and I found our way back to each other.

As women, it's easy for us to get lost in taking care of everyone else until we lose our identity and what makes us uniquely us. You must love yourself first in order for someone else to love you freely. I hope, as you take this *Heated Ride* with the Hellions, you find it inside you to love, embrace, and find yourself.

Much love,

Chelsea Camaron

PROLOGUE

Prologue

Jenna

"Have you ever thought about life on the other side of the line?" my brother Julio asks his best friend Ruben.

"Every fuckin' day, amigo."

I press my ear harder to the bedroom door, listening to Ruben Castillo, the boy who has grown into a man right in front of my virgin eyes. Julio and Ruben have been inseparable for as long as I can remember. Ruben has grown from a scrawny boy with crazy hair that won't lay flat to a young man who is tall with muscles, long hair worn slicked back into a low ponytail, and devilishly dark eyes. The same young boy who once pushed me on the swings has grown into a man who pushes all the buttons of my hormone-filled teen body.

I sigh and lean against the door. I would love to have a life across the line with Ruben.

America, the land of possibility.

Hearing the sounds of them moving toward me, I jolt away from the door and scurry down the small hallway to my room.

Ruben is going to find a way out of the poverty of Mexico, and I can only hope he will take me with him. Who am I kidding? He doesn't even know I'm alive anymore. Well, he knows I'm alive, as in his best friend's little sister, but he doesn't see the woman I am growing into.

While I'm not a little girl in pigtails anymore, I haven't filled out like my friends. One day, I will, but by then, I'm afraid it will be too late.

I have watched him as the girls paw at him and he's gotten what he needed and moved on. Julio does it, too, but he's my brother; it doesn't cut deep into my soul to watch him sleep with every girl he passes by like watching Ruben.

"I found a way," Julio says as they exit the room.

"Really?" Ruben asks as they pass by my doorway.

"On a work visa. We can go pull tobacco for a farmer. When it expires, we stay and find someone to get us papers."

My heart drops to my stomach. Julio and Ruben … gone. I can't exist here without my brother. Our life is hell. My only saving graces are my brother Julio and Ruben.

I sink down on my bed before realizing the guys are right out front. Cracking my window just enough to hear, I listen as they make their plans.

"I've got two weeks to get out," my brother informs, and I fight back tears as I remember the fight he had with our parents last night.

Dad was drunk and looking for me. He had already slapped Mom around and needed another punching bag. When Julio stepped in and took the hits in my place, our father realized my brother was a grown man who took it hit for hit. That's when he told him to get out. Our mother stepped in and bought him two weeks to heal, as she said, but really, it was so she could sneak him a little cash between now and his time to go.

"What the fuck happened?" Ruben barks out in surprise.

I peek outside and watch my brother light a cigarette. I hate when he smokes. "My time has come. I'm a man now, and the asshole knows I can take him."

"What about Jenna? You gonna leave her behind with the devil himself?"

My heart flips in my chest that Ruben would think of me. Then dread rushes through me. If they leave, I will be at the hands of Satan in human form.

Our father is far from a loving man, and our mother is weak. In our culture, she falls in line behind her man. Our rundown trailer is nothing to boast about, but our mother has done her best to keep it clean as she raised five kids. Julio and I are the last at home. My sisters married at eighteen just to get out of the house, and now they have babies of their own. They call and check on our mom from time to time, but overall, they stay away. My oldest brother is dead. Gang banging caught up to him.

For a while, I was afraid Julio and Ruben would follow Juan, but they didn't. Sticking together, they have managed to avoid the pitfalls of life in the ghetto just over the line in Mexico.

When we see the tourists from America driving their expensive cars on their way through to some Spanish retreat, I want to laugh and tell them to stay home. Their country is full of amenities and freedoms we don't find here.

Sixteen and stuck, what the hell do I know, anyway?

Dread fills me. If they go, who will protect me from the thugs on the street? Julio and Ruben make sure I get to and from school unharmed by escorting me. If they leave ... I can't even handle the thought.

Julio's answer makes my heart drop. "I've gotta figure out what to do with her."

"If we go on a work visa, she can't come. They don't even let wives cross." Ruben shares the truth I already know.

We have heard the stories of the people who fail to get across. The tales of success are few and far between. It's worth the gamble, though. Everyone here feels that way.

"North Carolina, hombre. We get there. It's a strong tobacco state. Lots of hard working men are needed. Being that far north, there's less chance of anyone asking for papers than if we try to stay and work in Texas. Once we get a place, I can have Jenna come on a tourist visa. She just won't return," Julio says as if he has all the answers as he takes a drag from his cigarette.

"That's smart. We go away from the border and blend in better. We at least speak and understand English. Not many fuckers here can do that. Maybe that will help us, too."

"We've just gotta get by. With the money we would make, I could send enough to take care of her. They put us up in a place to sleep. I can eat cheap and send everything else back home. I'm gonna call my other sisters. I want to make sure Jenna has somewhere to go if it gets too rough."

My brother is always looking out for me. He could do this and not care one bit what he leaves behind. He would be free. Here he is, though, planning to take care of me from miles and miles away.

He continues with his plan, "After we get ourselves set up, I'll find a way to get her over. If Mamá would leave the bastard, I would take her, too. Gotta get out and now, though. I'll sort the rest once we are in the clear."

"Solid, amigo."

That is my brother. He's the only male left, so he will find a way to get our mother where he is and me, too. It's our culture. If Ruben hadn't lost his mother to a drive-by shooting last year, he would be planning a way to get his mom out of Mexico, too. The men know to take care of their women—from the mothers to the wives to the sisters. No matter how hard they have to work, they will provide a home. No matter how long it takes, they won't give up on getting me to them. The question is, can I survive until then? The answer is...

No, so they can't leave me.

ALL THERE IS

RUBY

E at. Sleep. Shit. Shower. Work. Ride.

Wash, rinse, and repeat. This is my life. When did everything become the same?

I walk into my home, and there is a part of me that wants to turn around and walk right back out the door. From the ghetto of Mexico to a double-wide with a black picket fence, I have worked my ass off to build a life for me and Jenna.

Behind the stove—making an amazing dinner, I'm sure—is my wife, my life, my 'Vida.' Her long, dark hair is braided behind her back as she studies the pan in front of her, humming to herself. Standing in the doorway, I study her. I study our life.

Thinking back to when it all began, this is everything I ever wanted: my woman having my babies, cooking our dinner, and all of this while being safe. I came to America for a better life. It hasn't always been that way, but it damn sure is now, so why do I suddenly feel like something is missing; something is different?

While there are worry lines on her forehead, I remember when her face was flawless. My best friend's little sister, my amigo from way back, somehow worked her way into my blackened heart. She filled every void I ever had as a boy and helped me grow into a man.

Ride or die, she has been by my side.

Through the bad decisions for an easy buck to the good decision to join the Hellions, no matter what, Jenna has been there.

I rub the tattoo on my neck: Vida—life. My heart beats for her. Thick and thin, she holds me down.

I step into the living room where I immediately step on a car little RJ left on the floor, and I can't stop the irritation that builds inside me.

When did my life go from dodging bullets to dodging fucking toys? Are we too comfortable? Is this all we have left? Getting wrinkles and raising babies?

Vida looks up at me and smiles the same smile she has given me for years, the one that still brings my cock to attention.

When I study her further, she looks tired. No makeup covers her face. She's in sweats and an old T-shirt I could swear each of our babies has puked on more than once. Still, she sees me and she smiles.

Her body has grown. She has changed. With the swell of each pregnancy, she grew and she glowed. After each baby, she got curvier. She isn't large, but she is no longer the tiny, no hips, tits, or ass woman she once was. No, my woman, my wife, my life has curves.

Smugly, I think, *Yeah, I gave her those curves. Every time I planted my seed so deep, I gave her curves.*

I make my way to the stove where I wrap my arms around her waist and pull her to me. I kiss her, and she opens, ready for my tongue to greet hers.

Now, this is the life.

She wraps her arms around my neck as she kisses me back.

I get lost in my woman's arms, in her mouth, and in her touch. No matter what goes on, I can always get lost in Vida. She's always had that power over me.

She pulls away, smiling. "I gotta cook, Ruby."

"Turn it off and I'll turn you on."

She pats my chest before turning back to her meal preparation. "Maybe later. The babies need to eat."

Babies, my ass. Our kids are now nine, seven, and five. They can wait thirty minutes for me to eat my wife, get her off, and get mine.

I move behind her and pull her braid to the right, exposing the left side of her neck to me. Then I lean in and suck … hard.

"I'm hungry for you." I nip at the spot I just turned a nice shade of pink. "Now," I growl.

She pushes her ass into me to get space. "I said not now, Ruby. Geez, I've gotta feed the babies and then move the laundry. I've been at work all day, and now I have a house to manage," she snaps.

Barking back at her, I demand, "You have a dick to suck."

Her smile disappears. "Ruben Castillo, I don't have time for your nonsense right now."

"Nonsense? Take your ass back to Mexico where, when your man says suck his dick, you drop to your knees in the kitchen and handle that shit."

I went too far. I watch her eyes glass over in tears she refuses to shed. That's my woman: tough as nails. Any chance of getting laid went out the door, though.

I'm an ass. I can't help it. Things have changed. She

never has time for me. It's always our kids. I love them, too, but what happened to us?

She is the most beautiful woman in the world. I can't keep my hands or eyes off her. If I didn't have to go to work to pay our bills, I would live with my tongue or cock inside her tight heat for life. With each kid, though, our time together has diminished. Finding any little moment to hold onto each other is all I have. Here we are and she doesn't even want that anymore. When did she lose the passion?

I have heard of marriages having the seven year itch, but that couldn't be us. We have had ten years together. We have gone through more than the average couple, keeping each other's secrets when we were here illegally and then the stuff with her brother. Certainly, we couldn't find the place where we are in a lull.

I'm a motherfucking Hellion. Pussy is thrown at me constantly, but not the pussy I want. When did this happen? Where did the woman I married go? Where is the girl who couldn't get enough of my cock when we were mere teens?

When did everything change?

JENNA

Jenna

Take my ass back to Mexico … He has lost his ever-loving mind. He came and got me. Two years, I had to face my father's hand before Julio and Ruben came back for me. I saved every penny my brother sent, outside of what I needed to spend for food and clothes, so when I made it to America, I wouldn't burden them further.

Only, it didn't work out that way. I ended up in a two-bedroom trailer along with them and six other immigrant workers. As much as the money sent home could last, here in the states, existing is expensive. When one of the guys was looking at me a little too often, Ruben claimed me, and we moved out.

From the first kiss, I was lost to him. I knew, from the time I was a little girl, Ruben Castillo was the man for me. The moment he realized we were meant to be, my life finally began. From the moment Julio gave his blessing, Ruben hasn't been able to keep his hands or eyes off me.

He has this way of making me feel wanted, loved, and protected. One glance and my heart beats faster. My body is drawn to him like metal to a magnet.

It hasn't been easy, but we have built a life together.

After working the fields, Julio got Ruben tied up in some bad business.

A quick buck is always far from simple and money never comes easy.

When Julio took the fall to keep Ruben safe and, in turn, my life here, as well, Ruben vowed to be on the straight and narrow. One problem with that is, being in a country illegally is not exactly being on the straight and narrow.

Pregnant with our first child, living in a trailer with another Mexican family on the back side of a farmer's field, I was grief-stricken to know my brother was caught. And after serving his time for drug possession with intent to distribute, he was sent back to Mexico with no hope to return. Things were not good.

A chance meeting on the side of the road with Blaine 'Roundman' Reklinger changed our lives forever. Roundman was stuck with a blow out on his bike in the pouring rain. At the time, we didn't know he had help on the way. We just saw a man in a leather vest on the side of the road, getting soaked. Pulling over, Ruby got out and offered the stranger a ride.

"You fuckin' crazy?" Roundman asks Ruben as I crack the car window to our beat up Toyota Tercel to hear them.

"No. Just see a bike on the road that is obviously immobile and figure you might not want to drown."

"Good Samaritan's are a dying breed." Roundman extends his hand to Ruby. "Got brothers coming to tow my bike. Thanks for stopping, man."

Ruby shakes his hand and nods his head.

"What's your name?" Roundman asks as Ruby steps back toward the car.

Ruby raises an eyebrow at the stranger and walks away.

That rainy day changed everything.

Memorizing our license plate as we pulled away, Roundman tracked down the car to the farmer Ruby worked for, which led him to us. Almost ten years later, he's a fully patched member of the Hellions; we're legal citizens with education and jobs for us both; and we are so much better than where we came from.

Julio's sacrifice paid off. We send money home to him.

I miss him terribly, but I have this life thanks to Ruby and everything my brother gave up for us. At twenty-eight, I have three beautiful children:

Maritza, Mariella, and Ruben Junior. We own our own home. Even if it is a double-wide in a community of what they call modular homes, it's ours, and I am proud of it. I have a job I enjoy and a man I love.

Why he's being an asshole tonight is beyond me. Then again, when was the last time we had sex?

Since I took over at the mini storage office for Doll, things have been busy. My days were once spent passing the hours by cleaning, cooking, and caring for my man and my babies. Now I just can't seem to keep up. When my head hits the pillow every night, it's heaven sent.

As I think of how I have been neglecting my husband, guilt washes over me. He is my first priority, and I haven't been the best at taking care of his needs.

Swallowing the lump in my throat, I finish making dinner for our family.

The sound of the door shutting has my chest beating wildly as I continue setting plates on the table for my children. Tears fall when I hear the familiar thunder of his Harley cranking and then revving as he pulls away. Then my mind goes back to the moment we finally came to be.

"I'm never gonna be without you again," he whispers as he holds me close, breathing against my hair.

Safe in his arms with my brother in the living room,

I feel like everything that has been so wrong in my life is suddenly so right.

"Ruby," *I whisper back and lean into him.*

"I hated leaving you. I thought about things, Jenna. You being gone, us worrying about you, it gave me a lot of time to think. You're mine, Jenna. All this is for you. I know how you've been looking at me for years."

I gasp in embarrassment.

"You weren't ready—hell, you probably aren't now—but you've gotta know, Jenna, I'm not blind. I had to put space between us so I wouldn't take advantage of your innocence."

"Ruby, you know"—*I swallow, fighting my nerves*—"it's always been you."

"I know." *He turns me to face him.*

My heart beat races as my palms get sweaty. I can't focus beyond the thundering in my ears.

His head tilts, his eyes never leaving mine as his lips slowly find my own. Tenderly, he brushes his mouth against mine. I want to moan. I want to explode in pleasure from his simple touch. It feels like I have waited my whole life for this moment.

I open in a sigh, and he takes my bottom lip into his mouth with his teeth. He doesn't bite, but his hold has me tingling all over. When I open my mouth farther, his teeth release my lip, and his tongue explores my mouth.

Dancing, claiming, our tongues and teeth collide as

*the world spins around in my mind. Ruben Castillo, my
every fantasy, my one love is kissing me.*

*If I died right now, I would die the happiest woman
in the world. If this was my very last breath, I would
take it completely fulfilled.*

What just happened here? How did we go from not
being able to exist without one another to not being able
to be in the same house? I know things aren't perfect,
but surely, they aren't so bad he needs to leave, right?

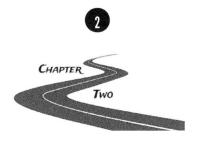

CHAPTER Two

RIDE IT OUT

RUBY

I take a pull from my third beer and lean against the bar. The clubhouse area is relatively empty. Then again, it's a weeknight, and there are no visitors from out of town or a party being held, so it should be.

"At the rate you're going, it looks like you're planning to stay tonight," Frisco states from his stool beside me.

I look at the bottle in my hand. Yeah, I guess I should plan to crash in one of the duplexes out back that Roundman has set up. Rules to the club: no drinking and driving. Roundman doesn't mess around with our lives like that.

I take another pull. My ass needs to be home with my woman. I have to find a way to make things right. Leaving was the wrong thing to do, but in the moment, I needed to breathe.

The open road soothes the soul: the feel of my bike under me, the power, the need to control, and the freedom of simply being. One mile after another, the air, the speed, and the drive give me the time to think. There are no bills, no babies, no wife, no house, nothing but me and my bike.

As usual, the ride led me to the Hellions' compound, the one place that has been home outside of Vida.

"I had an ol' lady once," Frisco says, turning to me. "She couldn't handle the life."

"Vida can handle anything I give her," I state truthfully. She will stand by me through it all.

The problem is, what if that's not enough anymore?

He slaps me on the back of my shoulder and grips firmly. "Brother, I can see that." He releases me. "Been here from the beginning."

I smirk at him and tip my beer to his patch. "You're

an original, man, so I know you've been here from the jump."

"Don't be a smartass, Ruby. I've seen a lot of women come and go. Few have the heart of stone it takes to ride out the unknowns. Vida, she's got that."

"Never said she didn't." I shake my head. "What makes you think my being here has a damn thing to do with my ol' lady?"

"A man like you wouldn't be away from a woman like that, otherwise." He smiles behind the gray-haired goatee he sports. "You can't keep your hands off her. She eats that shit up, brother. So tell me, why is your ass here, tossing back beer, when your kids are in bed and your woman is, too?"

"Things change."

"I never had a love like that, Ruby. I never had a woman by my side who looks at me like I am the only man in the world."

Anger builds inside me. "Looks can be deceiving."

"Ahhh, so there is trouble in paradise."

I huff. "I don't know of any marriage that's paradise."

Frisco pauses and looks to the wall in front of us. "That's where you're wrong, brother. Having a woman to ride or die with you for the good and the bad is paradise. There's no better feeling than knowing, day in and day out, you've got brothers; you've got family;

and when you lay your head down at night, you do it beside the soft, warm, sweet love of a woman who doesn't question when you gotta get lost in her, when you gotta confide in her, and when you gotta shut her out."

I raise an eyebrow at him. He makes it sound so easy. Day in and day out, it's far from easy.

"I didn't say it wouldn't take work. Loyalty like what you have at home is rare. A woman who is with you because she wants you as you are … Ruby, you've gotta know that shit just doesn't happen. They always think they can change you, tie you down with kids and life with them. Vida does her thing. She holds it down for you at home so you can be a Hellion, and she doesn't ask a damn thing from the club. All she wants from you is love and respect. What's not paradise about a woman who gives so much and asks for so little in return?"

I laugh out loud. He doesn't see. He doesn't live it— every day, the same thing on repeat. Sure, Vida loves me. She takes me as I am, the club, too. Lately, though, it's the babies this and the babies that, and they aren't even fucking babies anymore!

We crossed over from Mexico. We left our lives behind to be wild and free. There is nothing wild or free about our double-wide behind the picket fence. Paint it black, it's still a damn picket fence. American dream, is that what I've sold out to? The next thing I know, I will be wearing a fucking suit or some crazy shit.

"Fuck that," I mutter.

"Come on, Ruby, dig deep. You know you've got a good woman."

He's right. I have the best woman. Still, it just doesn't feel like enough. What the hell is wrong with me?

I take a long pull, finishing my beer and tapping the bar for the prospect to give me another. "Never said I didn't."

"Don't lose sight of what's right in front of you, brother."

"I know what I've got," I bark as I pop the top off my drink.

"Don't get disconnected from it."

"I have respect for you, Frisco. You have my loyalty. But, brother, you don't know what the fuck you're talking about."

He looks to the floor, the concrete beneath us, and says nothing. As I take another pull of my beer, we sit side by side in silence.

"Having an ol' lady is like concrete," he breaks the silence. There is a heaviness in the air, adding weight to his words. "The smallest cracks begin in the easiest of ways. A simple slip of a glass nicks the foundation. Whatever you've got going on at home, Ruby"—he looks up, and his eyes meet mine—"don't let the crack spread until it divides. Let me take you home; get lost in your wife tonight. Tomorrow, do the same. Whatever you're feeling, don't let it become a divide, brother."

I take in what he says. Get lost in my wife. That's what I wanted to do earlier today. She didn't want it. We have a nick, a breakdown between us. By being here, am I letting a crack become a divide?

Setting my beer on the bar, I nod to Frisco. Without a word, he grabs his truck keys from his pocket and we leave.

That's brotherhood: understanding what your brother needs, even when he can't see it.

JENNA

Jenna

Thank goodness the kids went to bed without a fight. I don't have any fight left in me.

In all the years we have been together, Ruby has missed more than one dinner, yet never ever has he come home and then left angry. We have spent time apart when he has been on a run for the club, but he has never avoided home out of anger. Although we have had our moments where we haven't gotten along, he has never left me. We also don't leave without saying good-bye. It's the biggest slap in the face he can give me without actually touching me.

Making my way through my bedroom and into my bathroom, I try to keep my emotions at bay. I have to be strong for my kids, for our family. Whatever is bothering Ruby, I have to let him sort that out and be the rock.

Washing my face, I look in the mirror. The lines on my eyes are from laughter, something I didn't have growing up. It's something my kids do without a second thought. We give them that. My babies have everything Ruby and I didn't.

I brush my teeth and think about the kids being due for their teeth cleanings. It's always something: yearly physical for school, sports, shots, or whatever. We get their teeth cleaned so we don't have to have major dental work ahead. One of them or all of them constantly have growth spurts. I'm pretty sure RJ needs new shoes right now.

Ugh, I will take care of that on my lunch break tomorrow. All day, every day, my mind is filled with so many tasks, needs, and something or someone needing my attention.

Spitting and rinsing, I wipe the excess off and put my toothbrush away. As I take my hair out of its braid, I look in the mirror. The vibrancy of my youth is long gone.

I brush out my long locks and hit my boob. I don't have large breasts except when I'm pregnant. The babies come and they swell. Then the children eat, and when the time comes, my breasts dry up, and they shrink back down. I have more than I did in my younger days, but the ever-changing size from one kid to the next has taken its toll, leaving them misshapen and sagging.

I tug at a knot in the end of my hair, the brush hitting my stomach, the very stomach that has grown with each pregnancy. I run my hand down the T-shirt and pinch my side. The extra skin I can't shed hangs as a reminder of the months of change my body endured to bring life into the world.

My babies, my Vida—life. They are my life. I was born to be a mom, their mom.

Looking up at the mirror, I study myself. What else do I have? What makes me … me?

The more I think about it, the more lost I feel. Outside of being Ruby's wife and the mother of his children, who am I?

I climb into our queen-size bed, the very bed that, night in and night out, Ruby has held me close. It's the bed we have made love in, the bed we have made babies in, and the bed we have shared everything in. Tonight, I climb in alone, wondering if I will wake up in the morning the same way.

Unable to sleep, I lie there, staring at the wall.

When I hear a truck pull up and stop in front of our house, my heart rate picks up. Ruby left on his bike. Please don't let there have been an accident. I was so rude to him. I shouldn't have pushed him away. I shouldn't have given up precious time with him. I should have turned off dinner and made time for my husband.

As the worst possible scenarios run through my head, I jump up and rush to the front door. I turn the knob just as someone is putting in a key and turning the knob from the other side. I pull as he pushes, and as the door moves, I see his cut and rush into his arms.

I pat his chest and cup his chin, feeling him. He's okay. Ruby is here in my arms, and he's okay.

Without letting him talk, I roll up to my tiptoes and kiss him. I need to feel him. I need to know that all the bad thoughts of motorcycle accidents and death that just ran through my head aren't real. I need to erase tonight from my brain.

I did wrong. He did wrong. Now, together, we make it right.

His kiss is fierce and his taste is a mixture of Ruby and beer. Now the truck dropping him off makes sense. I don't like when he drinks, but I'm thankful to Roundman and the club that no man drinks and drives.

As our tongues dance together, I don't care about earlier or even what tomorrow brings. My man is home safely.

His hands come around and firmly grip my ass, rocking me into him as he guides us backward. We hit the couch, and his hand comes up my shirt, cupping my breasts. The sensation of him touching me lights the same fire in me it has for what seems like my entire life. This is where I belong: under him, with him. Everything is me and Ruben.

"Vida," his whispers into my ear before he bites down on the sweet spot of my neck. "I'm an ass."

I stifle my laugh. He's right; he is an ass.

He pulls at the hem of my shirt, and I stop him.

"The babies." I pat at his chest in an attempt to move him. "Let's go to the bedroom."

Even in the dark of our living room, I can see the frustration in his features.

"Do you ever let loose?"

"We have kids; the time for letting loose left years ago," I defend as my mood changes from wanting to make love to my husband to wanting to crawl in a hole and cry.

Without another word, he pushes up off the couch before reaching out for my hand. Relief washes over me that he wants to help me up.

Hand in hand, we make our way to our bedroom.

Am I too uptight about the kids hearing us? How can I turn my mom brain off and give my husband my attention?

We get to our room, and I fully expect Ruby to pick up where we left off in the living room … Only, he doesn't. Helplessly, I see the entire mood has changed.

He pulls off his cut and shirt as he walks into our

bathroom. He will hang his cut on the back of the door and strip the rest of his clothes off, somehow managing to miss the dirty clothes basket and letting them land on the floor in front of it.

I sigh to myself. I don't know who is worse: my children or my man.

Climbing into bed, I ignore the ache in my chest of today's frustrations. I wish Ruben and I could be on the same page, but lately, I feel like we are so disconnected we don't even read the same book, and I don't know why.

Silently, my husband, my lover, my man slides into bed beside me. Just like every other night, he pulls me to him. When he tucks me into his side, he takes my knee and lays my leg over him before kissing the top of my head.

"Sleep, Vida," he commands as if he isn't pouting at me.

"What are you, two years old? Last time I checked, you were thirty-two," I say harshly. "Tantrums like a toddler aren't your style."

"I've gotta work tomorrow, Jenna. I've got kids to feed," he barks at me. "Sleep."

Just like with my children, I stop myself from arguing because it will get us nowhere. Instead, I lie in his arms and listen to the steady beat of his heart. Now

I'm the one pouting to myself for all the things I want to say yet don't.

When did we lose communication?

It's doesn't matter. As with everything else over the years, I will ride it out. Tomorrow is a new day.

STUCK IN A RUT

RUBY

W aking to her dark hair spread across my tan chest used to be my every dream come true. Night after night, Jenna would pass out over me after we had a passion-filled time, leaving her crashing.

I blow out a frustrated breath. When did it all get lost?

Once upon a time, I would have woken up to her

hair over my stomach as her mouth sucked me deep and hard. It was more than the physical. When did we become so disconnected? With one look, she could read me. In the last year, when have I had her attention long enough to even give her any kind of look?

I run my hand through her hair, and she stirs then looks up at me with sleepy eyes, tired eyes. The look makes my chest ache. When was the last time she got a break?

"Buenos días, hermosa," I whisper before kissing the top of her head.

She laughs. "I'm not very beautiful right now."

"Siempre."

"You are biased, mi amor." She looks to the clock. "The alarm is about to go off."

"Si." I continue to stroke her hair while she rests on me. "A new day, Vida," I say, hoping she can read between the lines and know that yesterday is behind us.

"Mami!" Mariella yells from outside the door.

The muffled sound of RJ beside her can be heard before he yells out, "Mami, Papi, it wasn't me!"

So much for a few moments in bed with my wife.

I laugh at my son. That is a telltale answer that he, indeed, did something he wasn't supposed to.

"Mami! Mommmmmm!" Mariella whines as I hear the doorknob turn.

Vida moves to get up, but I hold her to me. "No," I

whisper as two of our three children come to stand at the end of our bed, shoving each other.

"Momma is resting. Go on now and sort your shit yourselves."

"Ruby, language," Jenna sighs against me. "Hands to yourselves, hijos!"

"Go shower. I'll make them breakfast."

Surprise shows on her face at my offer. When was the last time I did this for her? The answer saddens me: never.

Reaching down, I squeeze her ass cheek before sliding out from under her so I can handle our children and give her some time to herself.

Scooping up my daughter, I carry her out of our room as I tousle my son's hair. With one last look over my shoulder, I am given the gift of my wife, my life, smiling at me as she lies back against my pillow in satisfaction.

Making my way to the kitchen, I set my daughter down as I look at the space in front of me.

"Maritza," I call out to get her to join us. If I'm going to do this, I need to knock it all out at once.

RJ sits down at his chair in our eat-in kitchen area. "Pancakes!"

"French toast!" Mariella immediately fires back.

"Chorizo and eggs," Maritza pipes in her request.

I say nothing, opening one cabinet after the next. Surely, we have to have it.

I smile, finding what I'm looking for, and pull three bowls down on the countertop.

"Fruit Loops," I inform them as I add milk to the cereal bowls and serve my kids. The looks on their faces have me fighting not to laugh. "I can't burn this," I tell them honestly.

"Mami likes for us to have a hot breakfast," Maritza shares with me, something I already know, but I don't cook. Normally, I don't go in her kitchen except to grab a drink or to sit down to eat. There's no way am I touching her stove. That would be the equivalent of her touching my bike. Hell no.

"Well, Papi made breakfast, so be happy he didn't try to cook," RJ retorts.

I don't know if I want to laugh or tell him to shut up. Kids.

"He got more than me," Mariella whines.

"I'm a growing boy," RJ defends, and I immediately want to go to work. Why must they argue over everything?

Making myself a bowl of the sugary circles, I watch my children, thinking as infants, they were life looking back at us: helpless, dependent, small, and ours to care for. As they grow, they have become little people with attitudes and opinions.

"Do you fight about everything?" I ask on a sigh as I lean against the counter and take a bite of my own cereal.

"Yes! It's his fault," Maritza replies, pointing to her brother.

"No," Mariella tries to answer, thinking she may be in trouble.

"They're girls; they don't get man stuff and want to argue all the time, Papi," RJ explains.

Shaking my head, I say nothing.

"Go get dressed for school," Jenna says, coming in wearing jeans and a T-shirt with her wet hair braided for work. She wraps her arm around my waist as our children each dump their bowls in the sink before going off to get ready. She looks into my bowl and laughs.

"A man's gotta eat." I scoop up another spoonful. "I'm just thankful we had cereal at all in the house. No way was I making pancakes or cooking anything involving eggs."

"You could have done it." She rolls up on her tiptoes and kisses my jawline softly. "I believe in you."

That right there … That is everything. She has always believed in me. I lose sight of that sometimes, and I shouldn't.

JENNA

Jenna

How does one's day go from exceptionally awesome to hell in a hand-basket so quickly?

First, before I even get to work, my phone rings with a call from Julio.

"Hola," I greet.

"Mi hermana," he says happily, brightening my day. "I'm calling because *I* am sending money to *you* this month. You can pick up the wire transfer today."

"Julio, why are you sending us money?" I question, completely stunned.

"I've got a good thing going, so I don't need your money anymore, and I'm doing well enough to send some back to my baby sister."

I don't want to upset him when he is obviously proud of being on his own two feet, but I can't help the nagging feeling that hits me.

Julio has a way of finding trouble.

"Julio—"

"It's good, Jenna. Trust me," he begs.

I don't have the time or energy to argue or question him further right now since I need to get to work. I will just take the gift at face value and save it in case Julio has a rough spot later.

"Good. I'm glad to hear it."

He laughs, and then we disconnect. After all, it's early for him in Mexico, and I have a job to get to.

Though the call should have been a bonus to my day, it leaves me worried throughout.

Next, I get rude costumers all day.

"Sir, I understand your situation; believe me, I do. The job market is tough. If you cannot afford your storage, then you had the option of emptying the contents months ago before you got behind. Now you need to pay your balance within ten days, or we will have to sell your contents at our next auction."

"Damn Mexican, coming to my country and robbing me of jobs and now my stuff," Mr. Falcon barks into the phone at me.

I swallow the lump in my throat. I'm an American citizen. I spent months and the Hellions spent the money going through all the proper processes to get papers for me and Ruby so that we couldn't be forced out of this country while our children, who were born here, stayed behind. Sure, we could appoint a guardian or take them with us, but the sacrifices we made were so we could have a family and future here in America.

I did not rob this man of a job; I was hired and get paid by the hour for the work I do. Why does he make assumptions? Sure, I may not have done it the right way from the beginning, but Ruby and I made it right with the club's help. If this man only knew the hell I left behind … Not paying for storage was the least of my concerns where I come from.

"I'm not robbing you of anything. You signed the contract. You made the commitment to pay your bills. We have provided our services to you and are due our payment. If you cannot pay, we will follow through with the terms set forth in the certified letter you received."

There is a click then silence.

"Mr. Falcon?"

No reply.

I hang up and make the notes in his account of our conversation. Seriously, he has had months and multiple letters and calls, so why wait until he is this far behind? Then, to make it my fault … People need to learn to have more accountability. I'm doing my job, plain and simple.

My cell phone pings with a text from Pami. We have gotten close since she moved here with her kids. They stayed with us while she made the transition from

Catawba to the coast to be back with them. It's been nice having boys around for RJ to play with.

Lunch?

Not today. Paperwork.

The amazing friend she is, my phone pings back, *I'll get the kids from the bus and keep them. Work as late as you need to.*

TY. I owe you one.

Never, babe.

I smile, knowing I can stay a little while longer today and finish up late letters and over-locks.

My kids love being at Boomer and Pam's. Her mother is there to be a grandmother figure to my children since they don't have any.

When Doll offered me this job a few years ago, I never thought I would be so happy to work outside of my home. My whole life, all I ever wanted was to be Ruben's wife and the mother to his kids. Then I was given this job that has been the best of both worlds. I get off early enough to be home with my kids afterschool, but I still get to make money to help afford things for them.

Ruben and I don't live off any government assistance and never have. We have felt blessed just to be in this country and didn't want to take anything more.

Taking a short break, I heat up some taco soup in the

microwave for lunch. Only, in removing it, I didn't expect the container to have gotten so hot, so it burns my fingers, causing me to drop it. The liquid splashes down my shirt and pants before spilling to the floor.

Cleaning up the mess, I lose time that should have been spent working, so it's a good thing Pam is keeping the kids afterschool. I wash out my clothes as best I can in the bathroom sink then sit in wet pants and a shirt for the rest of the day while I get all the payments processed and late accounts called.

The work day ends, and I get in my van to go home. There is a light on the dashboard lit up that I have never seen before. Ruben is a mechanic, so I don't give it much thought. I will tell him about it later and let him do what he does.

Stopping by Pam's, I pick up my kids, and then we head down the street to home.

Pulling in, I can't help letting the sense of pride wash over me. Ruben and I have done it. We are living the American dream. Sure, it took the help of the Hellions, but here we are.

"One at a time, while Mami makes dinner, tell me about your day. Go ahead and take your shoes off."

"Ouch," RJ whines.

"Stop hitting your brother," I answer automatically as I head into my room to change clothes before starting dinner.

"We didn't touch him," Maritza proclaims.

"It's my shoes."

I turn to watch my son struggle to get his shoes off.

"They're too tight."

Kids never seem to stop growing.

I look to Mariella who is wearing a shirt that, every time she moves her arms, an inch of her belly shows. I guess more than one of them has had a growth spurt lately. Add shopping for clothes to my to-do list.

"Okay, I'm sorry for assuming. Now, go and wash up."

"You know what they say about assuming," Ruby says, walking in. I was so distracted by my mental to-do list I didn't hear his bike pull up.

I smile at my husband as he makes his way to me. Wrapping his arms around me, he drops his head to mine and kisses me, and I allow myself this pleasure. He's been good to me despite my crappy day. He has been my highlight.

"Today, we had chicken nuggets for lunch in the cafeteria. Well, Joanne's were still frozen when she bit into one," Maritza spouts off, breaking the moment with Ruben.

Ruby smiles down at me. "Good thing your mother packs lunch for each of you, then."

"Yeah, 'cause they serve peas at the cafeteria, and

Logan says they have bugs in them because they are squishy," RJ adds.

I laugh. "You hate peas, and they are squishy when cooked, so it has nothing to do with bugs."

Heading to my room, I change into sweats and an old shirt so I can go to the kitchen and make empanadas while my children share their day with me and my man watches TV. This time is the best part of everyday—all of us together.

All of the wrongs wash away into this moment of being right—one happy family.

NOT DOING MY JOB

RUBY

A fter a delicious meal and a few bedtime stories, all three of my children are finally fast asleep. My woman is in my bed, in my arms, and today hasn't been so bad overall. It still feels like *Groundhog Day*, but how can I complain?

Jenna kisses my chest, and I squeeze her ass. She

then slides over me, and my dick comes to life. Her hair cascades over my face as she brings her lips to mine.

"Vida," I growl as I bite her bottom lip.

"I've been neglecting my man."

I rock my hips as I take her thighs in my hands, making her straddle me in just the perfect spot. She fits over me like we were made to go together. Her beauty is ageless, and her body is still my every fantasy. The longer we are together, the more I find myself wanting her and needing this physical connection to her—Vida and me linked together as one.

She leans up and removes her shirt then slides down my body, making my dick painfully hard and ready to be deep inside her. I slide her pants down over her ass, her helping to take them off, before removing my boxers. I then scoop her up to have her sit on my face, something I need to do before burying myself in her. She laughs, just to have it cut off as I dive in, feeling like I have died and gone to heaven.

With my thumbs, I part her pussy lips, licking back to front and front to back before I dip my tongue inside, rubbing the crease of her thighs to her pussy with my fingers. I have her muscles relaxed as she presses against the wall to keep her balance.

My teeth graze her outer lips before I suck on her clit and fuck her with my tongue. I can tell she gets lost in the moment as she grinds against my face, making me moan, which sends vibrations through her, causing her to rock hard against my face and roll her hips in a circle.

"That's it, baby. Find it," I whisper as I use my thumbs to part her lips again and blow against her, sending her sailing.

I suck her through her aftershocks, leaving her legs shaking around my head before she comes back down to earth and slides down me, guiding my hard length into her wet heat where she immediately tightens around me. I struggle, fighting the urge to roll her over and fuck her senseless. My girl made her move tonight, so I will let her have her play.

She's riding me, rolling her hips, rocking me into her sweet spot. This moment, this feeling, this is how it should be. Lost in each other, not drowning in the day to day activities. I crave this connection. I need it like I need air to breathe.

Her nipples point, and I pinch them before leaning up to suck them.

"More," she calls out.

Nipping her collarbone, I thrust up, going deep, giving her all I can. Skin on skin, I get lost in the sensations as she moves her hands to lean against my thighs, stretching back. Her head falls back, her hair tickling as it brushes my legs.

I watch a few moments as my cock moves in and out of her pussy before reaching between us and rubbing circles over her clit as she moves her hips, working herself to oblivion.

I still then push up, sending her over the edge, hearing her cry out before she leans over and kisses me.

Sitting up, she smiles as I thrust, ready for my own climax.

"Ruby," she says breathlessly.

"Vida." I smile back as I grip her hips, sliding her up and down my throbbing cock.

"We have to go shopping tomorrow after work. The kids need clothes."

What the ever-loving fuck?

When I flip her to her back without sliding out, she laughs, but I'm irritated.

I grab under her knees and push her legs up. Throwing her ankles to my shoulders, I bottom out inside her and still while she wiggles, trying to get me to move. However, I'm remaining steadfast.

"You feel me? You feel me inside you, Jenna? When your man is making love to you, it's you and me. You feel anyone else here? Me and you," I say firmly. "No kids, Vida. No one else. Me and you. Ride this shit out." I slide slowly in and out of her as her eyes widen in real-ization of what she did.

She bites her bottom lip, nodding her head as she starts building again.

I go deep, and she moans.

"Feel me, Vida. My life, your life, our life. Life, love." I slide back and rock in again.

She tightens around me, and I feel the tingle up my back as my balls tauten.

I run my hands up and down her legs as I increase my pace. "Get there with me, baby. One more."

She cups her breasts and rolls her nipples between her thumb and first finger as her inner muscles work me. Thrusting three more times, I release inside her and move her legs off my shoulders as I lean down and kiss my wife. She rocks up as I thrust through the last of my orgasm, and then she pulls away to breathe as her final climax claims her. Slowly, I move out of her and sigh.

I can't believe she tried to talk to me about our kids while we were having sex. I'm losing my touch if she can think about anything except me while I'm balls deep.

The same question I keep coming back to haunts me again. Is this what we have come to? Talking about kids during sex? When did we lose the passion?

Lying side by side, I look at my wife. She's still just as beautiful as the first time I lay in a bed with her. Regardless, I could roll over and go to sleep right now. Morning will come, and I will get up, shower, go to work, and be fine when there was a time I hated getting out of our bed to even be away from her for a moment.

Where did it go wrong?

"It wasn't a power play," she whispers, her eyes studying mine.

I raise an eyebrow in question.

"The sex, the kids' clothes, I wasn't using my body for a power play if that's what you're thinking."

"Hadn't crossed my mind, Vida." And it hadn't. I'm so frustrated with our entire situation that I can't even wrap my head around it enough to put it into words. Things just aren't right, but I can't say they are all wrong, either.

She watches me. "It just seems like we don't see each other as much lately. I was thinking about the next few days and what I needed to do—"

"Stop!" I throw my hand up and climb out of bed. "Seriously, we're fucking and you're thinking about your to-do list!" I roar, stomping to our bathroom.

I don't know if it's the downfall of pride or just my ever-building frustration with myself and my life, but I can't even look at her right now knowing that, in the most intimate of moments between us, she was in her head, working through her own fucking schedule.

It is complete bullshit.

I slam the door and get in the shower. I need to get out of here before I say something I shouldn't.

Jenna

Something isn't right. I can't put my finger on it, but there is a disconnect between my husband and I. The kids needing clothes wasn't the best thing to bring up after he gave me two orgasms and hadn't gotten his yet, but it hit me in the moment and I needed to tell him. My mind goes back to one of the first times we had sex.

"Vida, close your eyes, close your mind ... Feel me, Jenna. Feel me from the bottom to the top." He slides his cock slowly and delicately in and out of me.

I smile softly up at him.

"Esto somos nosotros, mi amore. This is us. We are one, me and you." He slowly moves, sending tingles throughout my entire body. "Don't ever play games with me with your body, Jenna. Sex is not a power play. You and I, we make love." He rests his forehead on mine,

locking his eyes to mine. "This is us, my love, my life. Take your mind away from everything else and just be here with me." His hand trails up and down my side, tickling and teasing as he uses his other arm to support his weight. "Nosotros,"—us—he whispers over and over before he drops his lips to mine and kisses me.

Closing my eyes, closing my mind, I allow myself to become one with him, lost in the moment, in the sensations, in our love.

It wasn't a power play. My mind is constantly racing because of three kids who always need something. I can't turn it off anymore. I can't help thinking of the next task. Everything is about the next moment, the next thing. Some days, it seems like I function on autopilot, just moving from one task to the next.

Doesn't he understand? As my partner, my spouse, my best friend, can't he see? It's not just us anymore. We have these children who depend on us. They grew in my body. For months, I sustained them. The moment they came into our lives, it wasn't Ruben and Jenna Castillo anymore.

There are plenty of times I wish I could turn it off, but I can't. I was made to be their mother. The moment I felt my breasts tingle from the new life growing inside my body, I was never the same again. I found my place, my purpose. There is nothing more important to me than my children. I can't turn that off, and I don't want to.

Letting Ruby pout in the shower, I grab my clothes and make my way to the kids' bathroom to clean up. What should have been an amazing night has turned into a bitter time in my marriage. How can he not understand where I'm coming from?

Lying back in bed, I turn my body to face the wall and fight to fall asleep. I don't move when Ruby gets in bed. He doesn't grab me like usual and move me to him. Therefore, I snuggle down deeper into the bed, fighting all the emotions dancing around inside me. I feel the bed dip as he turns from his back to his side.

In all the years we have been together, he has always slept on his back with me half over him. Tonight, I lift my head to find he has turned his back to me. My mind goes back to the first night I was in America.

"Jenna, we have to share the space. Tonight, you get me sharing the bed. Tomorrow night, you will have to share with Ruben. We will always let you have the bed and switch off taking the floor between each other. We've gotta work, hermana. It's hard work, so we've gotta sleep. Sorry, we aren't on our own yet, but soon," Julio explains as I lie in the full-size bed that practically fills the bedroom, and Ruben makes a space on the floor for himself.

Nerves have filled me all day while trying to get here. Now the time has arrived, and I can't relax. This is supposed to be a better place.

It took some time, but I finally fell asleep, only to spend most of the next day anxious about my first night sharing a bed with Ruben. Moving one of my pillows to my chest, I hug it as if it was the man I usually hold as I drift to sleep.

"Ruby," I whisper as Julio snores loudly on the floor beside us. "I can't sleep."

Two strong arms pull me close. He's on his back as he rolls me to his side. With my head on his chest, he grips my knee to wrap my leg over his. Gently, he strokes my hair until I fall sound asleep, feeling safe for the first time in my life.

Only, tonight, sleep won't find me. In its place is a new darkness in my heart.

I have heard the saying: *Never go to bed angry; that's the key to a lasting marriage.* I never understood that until this very moment.

For the first time since Ruby and I became one, I feel alone, even with the bed beside me being full. For the first time since falling asleep in his arms all those years ago, I feel fear. Worry is building inside me for what the future may hold for us. How do you work past a divide?

CHAPTER FIVE

5

FIRE

RUBY

I feel the bed dip when Jenna gets up. Her alarm hasn't gone off yet, nor have our children invaded, but she's up, which means she will get the kids' lunches made, breakfast ready, and then get dressed. Depending on what she has planned, she will pack herself a lunch or go out with Sass or Pam later.

I rub my neck where I have Vida tattooed. *Another day in paradise*, I think to myself.

Getting dressed, I decide I need a ride before work, so I make my way to the kitchen where I pause when Jenna looks up from the stove as she makes french toast, and I catch her glare. The kids are at the table, waiting for their hot breakfast while she and I have a silent confrontation.

The stare. The cold eyes, pinched lips, rise of the jaw, stare that says she is a woman hell bent on making me pay for the pain I caused her.

Yep, we have been together far too long; the glare doesn't even make me want to fix it. I'm numb, dead to all this.

Kissing my kids on the tops of each of their heads, I brush past Vida and leave. It's an asshole move, but I will not be led around by my dick if that's what she's thinking. The glare, the stare, the power of a woman's eyes is lost on me. Not today, not tomorrow, not anymore.

There was a time when her glare would have me stopping in my tracks to make it right. However, the divide between us is too great. I'm too frustrated with myself, with her, and with us to even try to fix this.

Climbing on my bike, I turn the key and twist the throttle, making it rev. The vibrations, the power, the sound, the beast beneath me is alive. The dragon inside me is ready to breathe fire.

Pulling out, I take the back roads to work, hitting every curve wide open.

"¿Dónde está el ardor?" I say to myself. "Where is the fire, the heat, the passion? I want to feel the burn again."

The air around me feels thick. The humidity has me wanting to yank off my helmet, my cut, and my shirt. A storm is in the air, and it's not the one in my house. There was a time when Jenna would have gone ballistic over me leaving without saying a word.

Pulling up to our small single-wide, I find trash bags of stuff out front. What the fuck? *I think as I park the car.*

When I go to the back door we use, I find Jenna with a screwdriver and lock in her hand. She drops the package as she focuses on what she's trying to do. The clang of her screwdriver hitting the wooden step sounds around us as I try to remain quiet.

"No mames," she mutters in Spanish slang, picking up the tool.

"Vida," I say, causing her to jump.

"Oh, he speaks," she fires out at me, continuing to fight with the lock on our door.

I laugh, and she stands from her squatting position to turn and glare at me. Eyes squinted, lips pinched together, chin raised in defiance, she stares, and my dick gets hard as hell.

"Ardiente,"—fiery, passionate—*I say.*

"Oh, you think I'm hot right now? No, amigo, that was eight hours ago when you left this house—our home —without saying good-bye. There was no rush, no reason. Do not, Ruben Castillo, take for granted what we have. You do not come and go as you please. This is not a motel, no-tell."

The more she gets fired up—the hotter she looks— the more I want to fuck her right here against the outside of our trailer for all the neighbors to see just how wild my woman gets.

I raise my eyebrow at her as I step up and put my hands on her hips. "That's what this is about?"

"Do not try to charm your way out of this. Your shit is in the yard, Ruben. If you want to treat this as a truck stop and act like I'm some puta, then let me show you where your stuff belongs." She crosses her arms over her chest as I grip her firmly. My dick is throbbing against my zipper with each word she says and every blink of her fierce, dark eyes.

I kiss her forehead. "I'm sorry, mi amor. You know you're my world, Vida." I take her hand and pull her arms apart, placing her fingertips against my neck where her nickname is tattooed. "My life," I whisper as she leaves her pinky on her tattoo and moves her thumb to stroke my cheek.

She pauses with her thumb over the gemstone tattoo under my eye. "My Ruby, my beauty in the ugly. Connected," she whispers as she touches the two tattoos simultaneously. I lean down and kiss her. Our tongues dance and our teeth clank as I back her to the outside of our home.

"Ardiente," I growl as I press against her. "I love your fire."

When was the last time she got fired up? Really reacted? She has packed my shit and put it outside more times than I can count. Yet, over the last few years, she hasn't fought me. No, she ignores me. I get the glare, and she spouts off at the mouth a little, but she gives up.

Where is the spirit of the woman I fell in love with?

I pull into a gas station, needing to top off and head in to work. The thoughts aren't solving any of my problems, so it's time to clear my head for work.

Cars—the pieces fit together to work. It's mechanics. There are no emotions involved. Things don't change. One piece moves against another to propel the automobile. If it's not working smoothly, you do some tuning until you find the right balance. If you need to spice things up, parts can be added to give more power. There are so many variables, and all of it can be taken up or down according to an individual's needs or desires. Marriage, relationships involve more than one person's needs, desires, and thoughts.

Taking off my helmet, I set it on top of the gas pump before dismounting my bike. Following the instructions, I swipe my credit card and go about my business as a little Mazda Miata convertible pulls up with two women inside. They occupy the pump beside mine.

The driver gets out with her skin-tight tank top, cut off shorts that leave the crease of her ass hanging out, and strappy shoes with thick heels that make her legs seem a mile long. Her long, blonde hair flows down her back in curls that she obviously spent a lot of time doing, only to get wrecked with the top down on her car.

Noticing she is having trouble getting the lever in her tank, I go over to assist her.

My mistake.

"You certainly know how to work a hose," she croons, tracing her manicured nails up my arm.

"I'm no firefighter; I don't play with hoses or hoes." I glare, but she only steps closer.

"Hellion, huh?"

"Pretty obvious, bimbo."

She smiles. "I could be for you." She steps even closer, her breasts brushing up against my arm.

I toss up my left hand and show her my tattooed ring finger. "Taken." I move to hang up the pump since I'm finished pumping her gas. When I turn around, she is right in front of me.

"She doesn't have to know," the blonde whispers, leaning in and pawing at my crotch. "I hear Hispanic men have elephant dicks." She blinks her eyes at me. "Huge, thick dicks." She licks her lips and shakes my junk.

I grab her hand painfully, making her whimper. "I speak decent English. Taken means unavailable." I release her wrist.

She smirks at me. "Your cock doesn't seem to agree." She looks down at the growing bulge in my pants.

I love a challenge. I get off on it. I'm also a man; if you stimulate a dick, it thickens. The blood will move to the extremity even if I don't want it to.

I blow out a breath and step back.

She reaches out and runs her fingertip over my name patch. "Ruby, hmmm?" She steps toward me. "A beautiful gem for a beautiful man."

"There's nothing beautiful about me, sweetheart."

She pulls at my shirt, lifting it to show my well-defined abs. Her nails dance down my stomach, making me flex instinctively. "We could be beautiful together, just for today."

I shake my head and step away. As nice as this is, as enticing as her proposition is, I can't.

"Name's Charlene. I work at the hair salon on fifty-eight. Come and see me any time." She winks. "I'll work you in and over."

Shaking my head and trying to reject thoughts of Charlene and being worked over, I put on my helmet and crank my bike. Then I pull away, trying to think of all the reasons I just turned down easy pussy. It shouldn't be this hard to come up with them.

I once heard that happy people don't cheat. When you are happy in your relationship, you don't think about stepping out. Well, I'm not happy in my home life, and I damn sure was tempted to fuck that barfly's brains out until neither of us could think about anything more than the next orgasm and whether we could really handle another round.

Jenna

He left and didn't say a word to me. I fight the fire of rage burning inside of me. My one pet peeve, my one request from Ruben, and he throws it in my face. He knows how I feel about leaving without speaking.

My biggest regret is Juan left and I didn't say good-bye. The day he was killed, I was fighting with him over something so dumb I can't even believe we were fighting. I wanted him to take me out that afternoon.

As the youngest and the girl, I wasn't allowed out without my brothers. Julio was off with Ruby, and Juan was going out to gang bang. I wanted him to stay behind and take me to the park, instead.

Looking back, it was dumb for me to even think he would want to go to the park with his baby sister. At the time, however, I had tunnel vision, thinking of only my own selfish needs and wants. My brother didn't come home that day or the next. Finally, one of his gang brothers told Julio he was killed the day before.

That's when the pressure was on for Julio and Ruben to join. The gang pushed and tried to recruit them hard, but the two held strong, focusing on their plans to make it to America. I didn't learn my lesson then, either.

I left for America, sneaking out in the dead of night. I didn't tell my mother good-bye. Fear held me back when I arrived safely, and I never called to tell her where I was. We weren't close, but she was my mother. I owed her the respect to say good-bye or at least assure her of my safety.

I did neither.

When Julio was sent back to Mexico, he reached out and was informed of our mother's passing—a heart attack, they told him. A broken heart from the loss of all of her children is more like it. I never said good-bye.

It changed me. Never do I leave my children or my man without saying good-bye. Ruben knows this. He can be as mad as he wants at me, but he doesn't need to leave without speaking to me. That is the biggest disrespect he can give.

I finish my morning duties for our children, all the while fighting back the urge to throw his shit in the front yard. Looking back, that was a lot of energy I wasted packing him up, knowing I would take him back. I don't have the time or the patience to deal with him today. I have kids to get off to school and a job to get to. If he doesn't want to speak to me because his male ego is still wounded from last night, that's on him, not me.

Like the strong woman I have to be for my kids, I push down my emotions and go about our morning as if I don't want to slap their father around and cut him. Again, I fight back my anger and frustration. My children don't need to feel the effects of my emotions when it has nothing to do with them.

After getting the kids on the bus to school, I get in my minivan and laugh.

This is not at all what I ever thought my life would be. Sure, I always wanted Ruben, but three kids and a house with a picket fence, driving a minivan … It's amazing and it's sad. I'm not even thirty yet.

Nevertheless, from the moment I first got pregnant, I knew this was the new me. This was going to be everything I was meant to be.

My life is no longer my own. From the moment Ruben and I created our first life together, it was going to be about our children. Today, years later, it is and always will be everything for my children. There is nothing I wouldn't do or give up for them.

I make the drive to work just in time for the rain to start. It's going to be that kind of day, I suppose.

The rain comes down in sheets, which keeps the

phone pretty quiet and allows me time to get caught up on the paperwork. My shift ends with not one word from Ruben. We only have our van and his bike, so it's not unusual for him to ride in the rain, but it's really coming down today.

I try to call him to see if he wants me to pick him up from work since he's just one building over, but he doesn't answer. He's either pouting like a child or working on a car. Either way, my day is done. I need to get to Pam's to pick up my kids and get home to start dinner.

Rushing through the drenching rain, I get in my van and start it. I pull away, not giving any thought to the light on the dashboard, the one I took the time to look up online at work today. The light warning me of my low tire pressure.

The steering wheel starts to shake, and the road noise of the tires changes when I'm about five miles from home. Finding a safe place to pull over, I get out to find my tire is flat.

"No mames. I should have told him about this." I look to the night sky, talking to myself. I'm on the side of the road, a road where people drive sixty miles an hour with a very small shoulder, and I have to sort out changing a tire. "Way to go, Jenna," I mutter to myself as I try to call Ruby again, only to have no answer. Then I dial Pam to let her know I will be late getting my kids.

"Hey, Jenna," she greets.

"I'm gonna be late. I have a flat on fifty-eight."

"You need me to send Boomer?"

I sigh as I fight back tears. No, I don't want her to send Boomer. I want my husband, the man who vowed to be by my side to do just that. Swallowing my pride because I need to get home to my children, I reply, "Please."

Without hesitation, she gets my specific location and hangs up after promising Boomer will be right there. While I wait, I send Ruby a text, letting him know my situation.

No reply.

I see red—fire. I am burning hot mad.

THE QUESTION

RUBY

"Thanks, Boomer." I end the call, thanking my brother for getting my woman off the side of the road and home safely.

Vida didn't answer when I called her back. I was working and didn't take a break to call her like I usually would.

It's raining cats and dogs as I make my way home.

Pulling up, my clothes are drenched, and my eyes burn from fighting to see the road in front of me. Then I look into the front yard, surprised to see she hasn't packed up my shit again.

I sit outside in the rain for a few minutes. I know there will be hell to pay when I walk in that door. Sure, I fucked up; I know that. I'm man enough to say I was a dick who pushed her buttons this morning. I was an ass to not call her back, too. I am a selfish prick for trying to provoke something out of her, all for me to find something I lost.

When she opens the front door so I can see the light from the house from behind our storm door, I know my time to sit in the rain is done. Her patience with me is done.

Climbing off the bike, I remove my helmet to make my way inside. At the front door, I'm greeted by Maritza holding a towel and RJ ready to take my helmet. I kiss my children on the tops of their heads before sending them off.

Jenna is in the kitchen, working on dinner. She says nothing. She doesn't look up and give me the stare. No, she remains steadfast in her task.

"I'm sorry I missed your call."

She turns away from me. "Boomer took care of it. Go and dry off and change your clothes for dinner." She is calm and collected, as if nothing has happened. "The children are hungry, and I don't want to make them wait any longer if we don't have to."

The woman I married, the woman I fell in love with, would have bitten my head off and threatened to serve me my balls for dinner for not being there for her. Who the hell is the woman in the kitchen?

I move to the bedroom where I remove my wet clothes, putting them in the hamper, hanging my cut on a hanger and on the shower rod, and then drying off and changing into some sweats. No shirt needed since, after dinner, I will watch some television before going to bed.

We move through dinner like every other night; only, she barely speaks to me and never makes eye contact. I don't know what is worse: if she went bat shit crazy on my ass or this quiet acceptance.

The kids go to bed … along with my wife. Mariella wasn't feeling well, so Jenna decided to lie with her until she falls asleep, but sleeping alongside her now is Vida.

What is happening to us?

Is there even an us left?

Frustration builds, leaving me tossing and turning all night. Morning comes and Jenna is in the kitchen, making breakfast for the kids like every other day. I fight the urge to throw my fist into a cabinet. Every day, it's the same damn thing, and she has settled into it.

She's okay with losing ourselves to the suburban dream. Where is the passion? Where is the heat?

Where is the life between us?

Rather than taking off for work right after breakfast, I stick around to talk to Jenna. I won't start something between us in front of our children. They haven't had to experience us argue, and they damn sure won't start now.

She gets the kids on the bus then comes home to find me still here. The surprise is in her eyes; but otherwise, she moves about her business as if I'm not even here.

When did it become okay to treat me like a roommate?

"Vida," I call out to her, and she turns to me while braiding her hair for work.

"Yes, dear." Her reply is cold.

"*Yes, dear*?" I smirk.

Patiently, she retorts, "Ruby, I have to get ready for work. I don't have time to fight with you."

Cockiness builds. "You got time to suck my dick?"

I was sure that would get a hair brush thrown at me, something. No, somewhere, the crazy reactions I have grown to get off on have disappeared.

"First, you must give in order to receive, and neither of us have the time for that. Go yank one out in the bathroom if it's that bad." She walks into the bedroom then comes out, carrying her shoes.

I'm angry. I'm lost. So I make a bad situation worse. That's what men do, my mom always said.

"I'll just grab a barfly and have her take care of what my wife won't." I grab my helmet and go to the front door.

Tossing a glance over my shoulder, I can see the pain in my wife's eyes as they gloss over in unshed tears.

She swallows hard. "If that's what you want, handle it. Just know what it'll cost you."

Walking out, I don't know the woman in my house. Hell, if another chick had looked at me twice, she would have gone crazy in the past.

"I'll cut a bitch, Ruben Castillo. You tell me how you don't share; well, I don't, either. You better tell that puta I'll slice her like she was on the wrong end of a drug deal with Los Zetas."

"Vida, I fucked her twice ... before you." I kiss her hard then pull away when she gives in to me. "It's you. She's got nothing on you. I'm yours," I say, smiling.

It makes me feel good that she wants to fight for what's hers. It's how it goes when you are in the gang life. She watched it with all the boys growing up. You have to fight for everything: territory, your man or your woman, your family, your gang, everything. Every day is a battle. My woman wasn't afraid of any of it as long as she had me.

Now, she's almost daring me to step out.

My phone pings with a text from Vida before I climb on my bike. I'm surprised as I read when I don't find her cussing me out or threatening to change the locks.

You're on your own for dinner. I'm taking the kids clothes shopping.

Oh, no, it's not going down like this.

I type my reply and hit send. *Name the time and the first store. I'll meet you there.*

I provide for my kids. If they need clothes, I'm going to handle it. She knows this.

Putting my phone away, I crank my bike and take off for work.

Jenna

I am drowning. I wish Julio were here to beat the shit out of Ruben for me. If he lets a barfly even touch him, I'm out. I do not have the time, patience, or energy to deal with this. We are married. This is supposed to be the time in my life when we are settled and we have trust and a life together.

Why is it all crumbling around me?

The day passes in a blur of me working while my mind fights my anger with Ruben.

Picking up our kids from Pam's, I meet Ruben at the mall to go shopping. It's easier with two girls and a boy to go to the mall where we can find shoe stores and clothing for all of them as well as dinner in one place.

"Pretzels," Maritza cries out as we pass the stand.

Mariella pushes her sister. "No, the stuffed cookies."

My frustration grows. "Enough. We will have dinner before we have anything."

Ruben leads us to a Chinese stand where RJ starts to whine about wanting pizza. Taking my son by the hand, I guide the children across the way to the pizza line at the mall food court.

"Must you give them everything they want?" Ruben chastises me in line.

I blow out a frustrated breath and move up to place our order, ignoring him. Pick your battles; that's my attitude. We have a night of shopping ahead of us, so why fight the food when I'm sure we will fight the clothing choices and the colors and shoes? When it comes time for the shoes that is a war in itself to find the right fit plus the look. It means trial and error of one pair after the next.

We eat silently as Ruby watches me. It's like he's looking for something, but I can't figure out what.

The girls' shopping is relatively easy. RJ needs new running shoes for school. Does he want running shoes? No. He wants boots like his dad's.

There was a time when I adored the way my son idolizes his father. Everything for Ruben Jr. has to be just like his dad. In this moment, though, with all the turmoil around us, it's hell. I need him to want shoes for recess and physical education class, not to ride on the back of his dad's bike.

I get that Colt, Wesson, and RJ have aspirations to be the next generation of Hellions. I'm good with it. The Hellions are a good club. They are the family Ruben and I never really had. Right now, however, I just wish RJ would be a little easier going about the shoes.

"RJ, you have to have running shoes. Boots are not allowed in gym class."

"So why can't I have both?" my son asks as if this is the answer to all the world's problems.

"We have to budget, hijo. We can't just buy you boots when you don't need them and you need tennis shoes."

"Give the boy both," Ruben pipes up.

I turn and glare. "Are you trying to pick a fight with me?"

When RJ grabs the box and heads to the register, Ruben pays without even giving me a second glance. In this moment, I feel like I'm losing control of everything.

After getting a few new clothes for the girls, we can finally leave.

Arriving home, I am exhausted. I go through the motions of getting the kids to bed and send up a silent thank you that tomorrow is Friday and we will have the weekend to relax at home. Ruben has a transport coming up for the club and leaves for the weekend.

Maybe the space is what we need.

Once the kids are in bed, I finally get to climb in my own.

"Gonna give your man some love before he leaves?" Ruben whispers into the space between us.

"I didn't even make it into bed, and you're already worried about your dick. Seriously, if you want love, do something to earn it."

"There you go, Vida, trying to use the pussy power play. Fuck that and fuck you, too."

Sitting up in the bed, I turn to face him. The light on the nightstand is on, showing me the cold features in his hard stare. I look at him. I stare, searching deeply. Where is the man I fell in love with?

There is a saying, *don't ask a question you aren't prepared for the answer to.* This is advice I should listen to. The nagging voice in the back of my head has been telling me to tamp down on what I'm feeling. I need to fight against the disconnect, but I don't.

"Ruben, what are we doing?"

"Not taking care of each other," he fires back quickly, too quickly. Things are on his mind, as well.

"Why?" I ask calmly. Somehow, even as I feel everything crashing around me, I find this strange calm in facing the unknowns that have been plaguing me.

He shakes his head. "We lost it."

Tears fill my eyes and begin to fall. The words tumble out before I can stop them. "Do you love me,

Ruben? Like, really love me? Not just as the mother of your children, but are you in love with me, Jenna Mariella Natera de Castillo?"

He hesitates, and in this moment, my entire world crashes around me. The train is barreling down the tracks to run me over, and I'm helpless to do anything except lie here and endure the pain.

It's funny how saying nothing is sometimes more of an answer than speaking. That is, until he speaks, and what I thought couldn't possibly get any worse does.

"You are the mother of my children…"

Oh, no, no, no, this isn't happening. He's not going to try to explain this away.

I hide my eyes and fight the tears, swallowing the sobs that want to escape.

"I will always love you, Jenna. In this moment, you asked, and I'm man enough to answer."

Again, he pauses, and all hope of fixing what's broken between us is gone. I know what he's going to say before he utters the words, but it doesn't make them hurt any less.

"I am not in love with you."

CHAPTER SEVEN

SET FREE

RUBY

In pain comes healing. Sure, this hurts, but in the end, we will come out stronger for it. Maybe, now that she knows, we can find where we lost it all and rebuild.

I look to my wife and what I see cuts me deeply without her even touching me. I held the knife, and I stabbed us both figuratively.

The woman I thought would fight to the bitter end for our family is dead inside. In an instant, I did that. I said what I feel as a way to start over, doesn't she see? I don't want anyone else, but no, I'm not in love the way we once were. The relief in telling her makes me want nothing more than to hold her; only, the look in her eyes speaks volumes.

It's the look of a woman who is crushed, and if I touch her, she's going to crumble.

The woman I married was strong. Nothing could break her. *Come on, Vida; find her again.*

I extend my hand to her, and she looks at it like I'm a snake ready to strike.

I think I made a bad situation worse. We have always said, if asked a straightforward question, we would not hold back from one another. She asked the question; I was real with my answer.

Taking her pillow, she moves from our bed. "I need space," she whispers to the wall, unable to look at me.

"I understand."

She pauses at the door to our room. "I don't think you do. I'll sleep on the couch. Have a safe run, Ruben."

Silence, darkness. She leaves me alone in our bed, the one we have made love in more times than I can count, the bed we made babies in. Now, it is the bed we lost it all in.

I lean back against the wall. What have I done?

Part of me thinks I should go out there and take it all back. The other half of me is so desperate for something to change I remain in place.

The night passes with me tossing and turning, still unresolved about my marriage and my life as a whole.

Is this a mid-life crisis? There are all the jokes of men going out and buying corvettes and motorcycles. Well, I don't need a fast car, and I have every bit of happiness in my steel horse.

The ping of my phone reminds me I have a bag to pack and a transport to ride along on. Therefore, I grab a quick shower then toss clothing in a duffle bag, and I'm ready to go.

Walking out, I am surprised to find Vida up and in the kitchen. It's early ... too early. Did she sleep at all? She has to work today. I don't want her to be tired and then have the kids by herself tonight. Making a mental note to call Boomer to check on her later, I move to the living room and put on my boots.

She doesn't speak, doesn't leave the kitchen. She continues about her tasks as if I'm not even here.

Standing, I go to her, and she doesn't move. She faces the wall with a half-made sandwich on the counter in front of her.

I stand behind her, holding her hips, and inhale,

taking in the fruity scent of her shampoo. "Vida," I whisper. My chest aches at the pet name I have called her for so long.

From the first kiss, the first moment we shared as more than friends, she changed everything for me. She woke up something inside of me I never knew I could feel.

Suddenly, the girl in my arms isn't Julio's sister. Jenna is a woman, a beautiful woman.

As she looks up at me, licking her lips, they call to me. I drop my head and brush my lips to hers. My heart beats faster as her mouth opens, and I seek entrance she willingly gives. Her tongue touches mine, and I see white, I feel heat. There is a hunger inside me that I have never felt before. I pull away and look into her eyes.

"Vida." I brush my lips to hers. "You give me life, Jenna."

I never felt anything before her. I was numb, simply existing, going through the motions. It's funny how things seem to come full circle. Somehow, I lost my wife, my Vida.

I grip her more tightly, wishing I could go back in time and figure out where it all went wrong. However, my phone pings, and there is no time. Tank is waiting, and I have a job to do.

I kiss the back of her head since she won't turn around. "I've gotta go."

"Be safe, Ruben." Pain is laced in each word as I sense her fighting back her own emotions.

I push away and head to the door, and my hand is on the knob when she speaks again.

"If you love something … let it go. Ruben, you're free."

I should stop. I should turn my ass around and fix this. I should do something, anything but walk out the door. Yet, do I listen to the voice in the back of my head? No, not one bit. I walk outside without giving her a second look back, too afraid of what I will see.

The heaviness in my chest weighs me down as I mount my bike and take off for the compound. Tank and I have a transport to Florida. It's a small shipment of gym equipment going to Marco for a mixed martial arts gym. Apparently, Marco's Boys are getting some upgrades. We watched them fight a while back when we were on a different run in Florida.

The energy during the fight was electric. Tank wanted to jump in and beat some ass for Sly. I got amped watching Huck fight. It's a shame he's only training now. No more fights. Great guys and badass fighters. It will be good to go down and get my head out of my ass for the weekend.

I climb into the truck's cab with my mind reeling. *If*

you love something, let it go. What the hell does she mean by that?

I send a text to Boomer to check on Vida later today for me. His reply is exactly what I thought he would say —he already planned to. The Hellions are family. They will make sure she's taken care of while I'm away.

"Wanna talk about it, brother?" Tank asks not long into our drive.

I smirk and continue to look out of the windshield. "What makes you think I've got something to talk about?"

We are men, bikers at that, so we don't talk about our feelings, our problems. Unless it's about beer, boobs, or banging, we don't have much to say.

"You've got that look, Ruby."

I give a half laugh. "What look is that, Tank?"

"The one that screams you're deep in thought."

The space around us feels smaller. I don't want to answer. I don't want to admit I left behind my woman after I broke her heart. I don't want to tell him I'm pretty sure I shattered the life we built together. More than that, I don't want to tell myself I may have fucked up everything, and I'm not sure if it really was a mistake. I have never been so confused in my life.

"Just shit on my mind."

"The kind that can drive a crazy man sane?"

I run my hands through my hair yet don't answer.

"The woman at home on your mind?"

I look to my brother in the driver seat. He's been through hell and back. He knocked on the devil's door and came back to life. It was a hard battle to get things back on track for him and his ol' lady Sass. They weren't even together when he took six bullets to his body and lay in a coma. She moved on, found a new life … away from the club. He fought back the darkness to live in the light with her now.

Jenna and I didn't have that. We have always had an intense love and passion, but once she came to America, it was me and her. There was no crazy push and pull; she was it for me, simple enough.

I look to my Hellions' brother. We have a long ride ahead of us, so I might as well talk, I guess. "Ever stopped and wondered if there is more out there?"

Tank stays silent for a moment, just looking out at the highway in front of us. "There was a time before I got shot when I was always looking for something better, never satisfied. I had the best woman for me right in my arms, yet I let that get away. I wasted time and had to fight hard to get her back. When you've got it, you've just got it. Don't go borrowing trouble."

"I'm not. I just don't know what's what anymore. She's good; we're good. I can't complain. The fire, the heat, it's gone. What if there is more for me, for her, for us?"

"Brother, you've got good at home. Not many women can handle our world. Don't go borrowing trouble."

Borrowing trouble. No, I already bought myself a shit storm of trouble at home.

JENNA

Jenna

oy fuerte—I am strong. I keep telling myself that, anyway. Maybe, if I repeat it enough in my mind, it will come true. If you speak it, you breathe life into it.

"Soy fuerte," I whisper to the kitchen wall.

I can do this. For my children, I will do this. Years ago, long before I ever had children, I promised myself that they would not live in a house of fear, a house of anger, and a home with no love. Ruben is a great dad, and he can still be without being forced to stay in a loveless marriage.

I spent my night sitting on our couch, crying. It's old and worn out; there are stains; there are frayed edges, but this piece of furniture tells a story. The peg in the back corner that replaces a lost couch leg keeps it level —we knocked it off while trying to move it into our first home together. In its cushions are the long ago memories of movies watched while cuddling. My mind goes through it all: Maritza using it to pull up when she first tried to walk and the cushions sliding off, making her fall; the nights up with RJ colicky and the only thing to soothe him was me sitting upright with him against my chest—no movement, just me and my baby boy; Mariella flipping herself around as a toddler and doing headstands. Each home, each baby, and each moment, this couch has weathered them all with us. It's battered and beaten, but it's strong and held us up through everything.

I trace the seam of the arm. Can I survive the storm around me? Sometimes, when we can't see the light at the end of the tunnel, we simply have to do the next thing.

Ruben is gone, on the road for the club for the weekend. I have two days to sort my life, my future, and most of all, my kids. Lunches are already packed, so I just need to wake them up and feed them breakfast.

Having a moment to myself, I call the one person who has been by my side even before Ruben.

"Hermana," Julio answers groggily. I didn't think about the time difference in Mexico when I dialed.

"Julio, I'm sorry. I'll call back later."

"No, talk now. ¿Qué pasa?"

I sigh, needing to just get it out. "Ruben and I have had this awkwardness between us for a while. Then, well, I guess it all just blew up. Se terminó entre nosotros."

His tone changes. "What do you mean, it's over between you two?"

I fight back a sob. "He's not in love with me anymore."

"I'm gonna fuckin' kill him."

"Julio, no, no." The tears are falling as I beg my brother to calm down.

"He hurt my hermana. I trusted him with you. He broke his promesa. Do you get that?" I can feel my brother's rage through the phone.

"I didn't call for you to get angry. I called for support. Just tell me I can do this."

He blows a breath into the phone. "You can do this, hermana. You *will* do this. Your kids will have what we didn't. They will have a life of stability in America, raised by a mother who is strong. Ruben has made his bed and lost the love of a strong woman. You will be more than okay, baby girl; you will be better for it."

He always knows just what I need to hear. "I love you, Julio."

"Back at you, hermana. No more tears."

After a quick good-bye, we disconnect since calling isn't cheap.

No more tears. I'm not going to cry anymore. There comes a point when I have to face my new reality.

Crying isn't going to change anything. Sometimes, when things get bad, you simply have to do the next thing. I have to find a way to keep going until I come out on the other side.

I finish getting myself ready to deal with my children.

The ding of their alarms go off as I rub my eyes once more. Looking to the ceiling, I send up a silent prayer that my babies won't notice I was up all night, crying. I have to be strong for them. They didn't ask for any of this. Adult problems are not children's problems. This is between me and Ruben, about me and Ruben, not them. I blow out a breath and stand.

Making my way through the house, I wake each of them then go to my room to get changed.

I fight back my tears in the closet where his clothes are hanging freely beside mine. They are waiting for his return. They are here as if last night never happened.

He hesitated. Before he even said the words, the pause was all I needed. When you are in love with someone, there is no question, no doubt. There is a difference between being in love and loving someone. Till the day I die, I know Ruben Castillo will love me. I gave him three, beautiful children. We have survived thunderstorms in life together, and until now, we have come through, back into the light of a new day.

I run my hand over his shirts, stopping when I get to

my section. My clothes hang behind my man's. How many times have I stood behind him blindly? How many years have I been Jenna Castillo, Ruby's ol' lady? How long have I been his support? And where is mine?

Anger builds alongside the hurt. I can do this. I will not stay with someone who isn't in love with me. I want my children to see the love in their home. I want my girls to know what a healthy relationship is. I don't want to raise them to believe they stay where they aren't wanted just to fit into some mold. That is a recipe for disaster, one I won't set my children up to experience if I can help it.

After dressing for work, I finish getting the kids breakfast then send them off to school.

On the drive to the office, fear hits me like a sledge hammer.

If Ruben and I aren't together, where do I fit in with the Hellions? He's the patched member. Woman are only part of the club by their association to their men. I'm his ol' lady, his property, his responsibility. Everything I do represents my man. Only, he isn't my man anymore.

I get to work and start my daily tasks. The more I think on everything, the more I realize I probably should pack my desk. Maybe I'm being dramatic and taking things too far, but I can't help it. I'm a mom, and I have to know where I stand with my job so I can provide for my kids. Ruby isn't in love with me anymore.

I let those words sink in. Ruben is not in love with me.

Finding a box, I begin to fill it with my pictures and personal belongings. I don't have a ton here, but I have accumulated some stuff over time.

As I pack each item, I think on how comfortable I have become here.

Comfortable.

If I had to describe everything in my life lately, that word comes to mind. Is that where it all went wrong with Ruben and me? Did we become too comfortable?

The bell on the door chimes, and I turn around to see Blaine "Roundman" Reklinger walking in the front door. His long hair is braided down his back, his goatee trimmed, and his president patch on his cut rests over his black T-shirt with jeans and black boots. Roundman is tall, built, and has a look that screams intimidation.

His deep, raspy voice cuts through the quiet of the space. "Got something to tell me, Vida?"

I open and close my mouth like a fish, no words coming out. What can I say?

He points to the box on my desk. "Going somewhere?"

As tears fill my eyes and threaten to escape, I look down at the floor, fighting them back before taking a deep breath and trying to explain. "Ruben and I are…" I can't say it. "Well, we … um … I'm not sure I'll be working here any further, so I—"

"You what? And why the fuck aren't you sure about working here? Do you need a raise, time off, some shit like that?"

I put the back of my hand to my forehead, pushing to keep the tears at bay. "Ruben and I are … We're having some problems." I pause, trying to find the words.

"What's that got to do with your job?"

I look up at the man, and he looks back at me in all seriousness.

"Vida, I don't give a shit what you've got going on at home unless you need me to give a shit about what's going on. You work hard, and I trust you, so if you want a job, you've got a job."

When the tears fall down my face, I look down to hide them. I need my job. I like my job. I have three kids to raise on my own. I have bills to pay, and I have never been on government assistance, nor do I want to start now.

Two strong arms pull me to him and wrap me in a hug. A sob escapes me as the cold of his leather cut presses against my face, and I let my tears run freely.

"Do I need to fuck him up?"

I shake my head.

"Ruby is a Hellion, Vida, but you're still family. If you need anything at all, you call. You two sort your shit proper. You've got kids. You've got a job as long as you want it. Don't ever doubt your place here."

I nod my head, feeling a small weight lifted off my shoulders. As alone as I should be in this situation, I'm not. Who would have ever thought the Hellions would still be my family even without my man?

Then again, patch or no patch, I shouldn't doubt the club. They have always been rock solid for us.

Us … That word is my kryptonite. It cuts me so deeply I want to crumble to the floor. I can't, though. I have kids to be strong for.

Pushing away from Roundman softly, I wipe my face with my hands and ready myself to get back to work.

He goes to his office where I hear him mutter to himself, "No fucking way am I doing that damn paper-work. I'm gonna have to pull Ruby's head outta his ass." He shakes his head as he closes the door behind him.

Rolling my shoulders back, I face the day. I'm a Hellion, too. Ride it out—it's what we do.

CHAPTER EIGHT

CAN'T TAKE IT BACK

RUBY

As we make our way to Florida, my phone constantly rings from Julio. I know what he wants, so finally catching a moment to myself, I return his call.

"Oh, you fuck up with my sister and suddenly become unreachable?" he answers sharply.

"On a run for the club."

"I don't give a shit. My sister is heartbroken and you wanna avoid me. Wrong move, amigo."

Anger builds inside me. "Don't you threaten me, Julio. Out of respect for our past and your sister, I'll let that one slide. Do it again and you won't be able to threaten anyone else."

"Punkass, I'm not takin' shit from you when my sister is the one you fucked over."

"Julio, it's between us, and you've gotta know I didn't mean for it to go down like that."

"You can't take it back."

Before I can reply, the call is disconnected. I try to call him back, but I can't get through, which happens sometimes.

The ride home after the successful transport is long. The calls back made the distance seem even greater. Jenna has been good to let me talk to the kids; but otherwise, she hasn't said anything. I can hear the pain in her voice. It kills me inside to know I caused it. I also wonder what exactly she told Julio.

He's right, though. I can't take it back. Even if I could, would it change anything? No. I would live in the same pattern. I would remain unhappy until I finally exploded. At least this way, Jenna and I can find a way to co-parent. She's an amazing mother to our children. We will work out what's best for them. In the long run, it will be best for all of us as we both find our happiness again.

Life is too short to waste with regrets. I started down this path, and we're going to have to ride this out, too.

We are locking the truck up in the back lot when Roundman comes to the gate.

"Good to see you're back," he greets.

Tank gives the Hellions' president the typical half-hug, back slap man greeting. "Glad to be home. If you don't need anything, I'm going home to my ol' lady and Red."

I'm sure his woman, Sass, and his son, Red are happy he will be home tonight. My kids will be happy to see me, but my wife, well, that's questionable.

He heads off, leaving me with our leader alone.

I give Roundman the same half-hug, back slap, but when he pulls away, he doesn't let go.

"Ruby, I don't know what's going on at home. I don't need to know. You've got a place here on the compound, though. Always."

I nod my head, not understanding how he knows anything.

Reading my face, he explains, "Gotta get your head outta your ass. Vida was going to quit. I told her, as long as she wants a job, she's got one. I don't know if your woman will still be at home when you get there, but if she is, let her stay. Don't make your kids move while you two find your way through whatever you've got going on."

If he would have punched me in the gut, it would have hurt me less than what I feel now. Will Vida be at home when I get there? She loves her job, yet she was going to quit?

"If she's gone, I can't make her come back."

"I was married once. Doll's mom was the strongest woman I ever knew. Being a wife to this life, being a mom to young kids, it takes its toll. Your woman is strong, Ruby."

I know about Roundman's wife. She died when Doll was still young. He doesn't say a lot about her, but he damn sure hasn't moved on. What does that have to do with Jenna?

"Never said she wasn't."

"A woman can only take so much. No matter how strong she is, she's still breakable."

Feeling the need to defend myself, I bow back and stand up a little taller. "When I left here, she may have been a little upset, but Roundman, that woman was far from being completely broken," I tell the lie to him and myself.

I know I killed a piece of her and a piece of us, but I don't know what more I could have done. She asked a question, and I gave her the honest answer. I'm lost; she's lost; and together, we lost it all.

Once he looks at me then releases my shoulder, he rubs his goatee as if he's trying to form the right words. "Treat a woman like glass. She's not fragile, but cherish her like fine china. Hold her close, hold her tight, and be mindful of all you do with her. Ya hear me?"

I nod my head, knowing he's right yet also knowing that doesn't fix my situation. Somehow, I have fallen out of love with my wife.

I rub my neck, my tattoo.

"Shit ain't right for you without her."

Looking to the ground, I kick the rocks around my feet. "Shit ain't right for me with her, either."

When he turns and starts to walk away, I follow. After a beat, he speaks up. "The way through life's road isn't always paved for us. Sometimes, we have to navigate through curves and narrow places before we can find our way to open highway."

I start to reply, but his hand comes up in the air to stop me. "Say nothing. Think on the road before you. Think on what you see when you think of the end of the road. If you need a place to stay here, you got one. If your ol' lady or your kids need something, just say the word, brother. We've got you."

"Roundman, thanks." I pause. "Thanks, and I don't just mean for this, but for everything all along."

"Long time ago, a young man and his young woman were in a small car, riding down a busted road in the pouring rain. My bike had blown a tire. I was waiting for Frisco and Danza to come back with a truck to haul her home when these strangers stopped." His eyes meet mine. "I laid her down that day. I had one of those moments when you crash and the world is falling around you. I sent the boys back and stayed so I could have a moment to put my head back on straight. I was drowning that day, but not just in the rain.

"Your path led you into mine. You didn't have to stop that day. Shit, brother, I can't say that, with my woman in the car, I would've done the same thing. Nevertheless, you did, and you did it with no expecta-tion of anything in return. That shows the man you are." He reaches out and pokes my chest harshly. "Don't get lost in the moment of today and forget where you came from and, more importantly, where you're headed."

Before I can take in all he's said or come up with a reply, he walks away.

Where am I headed?

Home.

Dread fills me. What will I find when I get there?

My path was meant to lead me to the Hellions. In the club, I found the family I lost when my mother died. I found brothers I never had and father figures who were better than the bastard who left me behind.

I brought Jenna with me. Julio and I put her on the plane and got her to us. We set her on this path. And now I have left her to find her own way without me. Is that right? Am I the man Roundman just described? I don't know. I shouldn't have told her what I was feeling. Surely, I could find a way to make myself feel again. Then again, what if I can't?

My life has suddenly taken a left turn on an unmarked road. I don't know if I'm coming or going. Roundman says don't forget where you're headed … However, I can't see beyond the moment to know what the future holds.

The sound of his Harley pulling up catches my attention. I know the day is here and the time is coming, but I am no readier for it than I was two days ago.

I want to run outside and cut his tires. I want to shove him, punch him, rip his nails off with pliers, and every other painful thing imaginable.

During the time apart when he's called, I maintained

my composure. For my kids, I made sure to keep things as normal as I could. They don't know what's going on, and I don't know how to tell them just yet.

As soon as the kids went to sleep each night, I sobbed into my pillow. Picking up the pieces is hard to do when I never thought I would have to. My entire existence has been wrapped up in being his wife for so long I never imagined a day when we wouldn't be together, when we wouldn't be in love. Yet, here we are.

"Papi's home!" RJ cries out, and his two sisters come from their room to rush to the front door with him.

Emotions fill me. The hard shell I have tried to build over this weekend is ready to crumble already. My entire world has crashed around me, and I somehow have to be the strong one who finds a way to be nice to him in front of my children.

He is and always will be my children's father. There will be a place in our home and in our lives for him no matter what. But how do we navigate this? How do we find a way to co-parent? Can we manage to co-exist?

Swallowing the lump in my throat, I, too, go to the door to wait for the father of my babies to make his way inside.

"Dame fuerza." I beg for strength to get through the evening.

Taking a deep breath, I open the door just as Ruben makes his way up the steps. *I am strong,* I remind myself as he looks at me and our eyes meet. There is a pain in the depths of them that I can feel as he makes his way inside our home.

Stopping in the doorway, he kisses the top of each of our children's heads. Then, making his way to me, he stops and kisses my cheek.

Awkward. I don't know what to say, what to feel, or what to do.

Whispering, I remind Ruben of our situation, "You can't take it back."

He steps back and just looks at me while I remain strong, fighting back my need to cry. Once the stone is thrown, it can't be un-thrown. Once the words are spoken, they can't be taken back. He can't come in here like nothing has happened.

"Mami made menudo for dinner," Mariella informs as she makes her way into the kitchen to finish setting the table, breaking the moment between us.

"Looks like I'm home just in time," Ruben replies.

I want to scream. Home! Does he really think this is home? Does he think we can simply move on after he told me he isn't in love with me? How can we have a home with no real love?

I watch as our children scurry to the kitchen to get ready to eat while he makes his way inside, carrying his travel bag.

Home! It burns deep inside me. Down to my soul, I feel the pain. How can this be home?

Taking his bag into our room, he surprises me when he doesn't come out in his usual sweats, but instead, stays in his jeans, T-shirt, and cut. We sit down without a word shared between us.

As he eats the Mexican soup, he looks to me with unspoken questions. What? Did he really think I would be the welcoming party?

Oh, yes, dear, thank you for returning from doing God knows what with God knows who. I'm just thankful to have you here. Please just stomp on my heart, kill the life we've built together, but as long as you make your way back, it's all okay.

He's smoking crack if he thinks like that.

Dinner passes with me barely able to eat. Then the children move about their nighttime routines as if nothing is happening.

Hold it together, I tell myself.

For them, I can get through this. I have held it together the last few days all by myself as I have tried to figure out my future. I can remain rock solid for them for a little while longer. However, once they go to sleep, Ruben and I need to have a very important conversation.

The one that begins with, 'It's over, so now we must find a way to begin again.'

CHAPTER NINE

Picking Up the Pieces

Ruby

"Jenna," I begin once the kids are quiet and I'm confident that comes from them being sound asleep.

She looks at me. Her once tired eyes look completely exhausted. I caused her that level of pain.

Guilt eats at me as I pat the couch beside me, hoping she will sit. However, she shakes her head and paces our small living room.

Pausing in her stride, she looks at me. "We have to find a new way to go on."

I nod, lacing my hands together, resting my elbows on my knees, and looking at the carpet beneath me. "What have you told the children?"

She gives a sharp, half-laugh that is sarcastic. "Nothing. I can't wrap my own head around it enough to have words to give our kids."

Looking up, I catch her gaze. "I'm sorry."

She blinks. "Sorry? You're sorry? Ruben, do you know how sorry I am?" There is sharpness in her tone, but she doesn't yell. "I have no idea what to tell the kids. I don't know what to do next."

I think while she stands there, looking at me for answers.

"Let's just try to see if we can get the spark back," I suggest, believing in all honesty that it could happen.

Tears fall down her face. "You think you're gonna live here when I know you aren't in love with me anymore? You think I can just forget it?"

"No, no, not forget, but we can work on things."

Tossing her hands up in frustration, she looks at the wall behind me. "Do you know what I can't let go of?" She can't even look at me right now, and I think that hurts the worst. "I can't get past the hesitation. You see, Ruben, it wasn't the words, although I must say those cut like a knife. It was the pause you took to think about your answer. If you asked me, 'do you love me?' without question, without fail, I could answer that, through it all, yes, I do. You couldn't do that."

Taking a deep breath, I try to find the words to soothe her. "What do you want me to say? I can't take it back. You know it and I know it. We're in this place, a tipping point. Maybe we can tip the scales back in our favor."

She puts her hand on her hip and stares at me. "Do you think I can work on anything knowing you aren't in love with me anymore? Knowing we had it and we lost it, and I can't even for the life of me figure out where it all went wrong?" She moves closer, never raising her voice. "For two days"—she holds up two fingers for emphasis—"two days, Ruben, I have sat here, racking my brain. Forty-eight hours, I have spent trying to find the thing I did wrong, the moment in time where it all fell apart. Do you know what I figured out?"

I stand and reach out, only to have her pull away, staying out of my grasp. "No, Jenna, I don't know what you figured out when I can't figure it out for myself."

"I am not the same woman you married; that's what I figured out."

Things look up. She can see where I'm coming from. I have this glimpse of hope.

"No, Vida, you're not."

"And you, Ruben Castillo, are not the man I married."

Well, if that isn't a blow to my ego as she throws my own hang ups back at me … She's right, though. I'm not the man she married.

She continues, "We grow. We change. We either do it together, or we do it apart. The time has come when we do it apart." The tears continue to fall, but the firm look on her face shows me she is serious.

"Is this what you want?"

She wipes her eyes with her hands and pauses. "What I want …? What I want is for my husband to love me for better or worse. What I want is to raise my children in a home where, day in and day out, they get to see and experience the real love of a man and a woman the way it should be."

"I want that, too."

"Do you really? The last time I asked you if you were in love with me, the answer was not in line with that. If I asked again, would your answer change?"

This is not anything like I expected my return to be. I stop and think. Would my answer change? I can't say it would. It's only been two days, during which I was gone.

"I don't want you to answer that question again," she continues when I am quiet for too long. "I don't want a lot of things. I don't want to feel less than. I don't want to simply be with you because it would be easier or it would take the burden of guilt off your back. I don't want to, as you say, 'work on things' and have it translate into me walking on eggshells around you, my husband, the man who should love me unconditionally."

Her words rock me, and I sit back down, dropping my head into my hands. "You want me to leave?"

"One of us has to. I can take the kids and stay with Boomer and Pam until I can sort something out for us. It's not fair to either of us to try to make this work when I can't make you love me, and I'm not going to worry about, if dinner isn't just right, will that be the straw that breaks the camel's back. I have too much to worry about with raising my children."

"*Our* children," I interject. "You aren't alone in this, Jenna. I'll still be here."

She looks at me, and I can see the fight in her. "You will be … for *them*."

I stand again and go to her. She doesn't move, so I wrap my arms around her, pulling her close. "And for you. I'll always be here for you."

She cries quietly while I hold her, feeling like I'm dying inside from doing this to her, to us. When she pulls away, I look down at her swollen, red eyes and fight back the emotions swimming inside me.

"I'll stay at the compound. You and the kids stay here. Lock up the house, and Boomer is down the street if something happens. I'll come back tomorrow after work. We'll figure out what to tell the kids, and I'll help you get them ready for bed."

She sniffles and nods her head in agreement. I guess we are getting somewhere, even if that somewhere is farther apart.

JENNA

Jenna

Oddly enough, having settled some things with Ruben, I feel like I am getting my head around all of this. At the end of the day, he can't stay here. We can't fake it until we make it. To do so wouldn't be fair to either of us, and it would only succeed in drawing out the inevitable. Our children deserve better than that.

Picking up his duffle bag, I move to our room. I'm not sure of the laundry situation at the duplexes on the compound, so I simply put his dirty clothes in our hamper like I have for so long. Then, opening the bag, I help my husband pack to leave.

I'm not sure what would be harder: packing my own stuff and the kids or packing him, knowing this is it. We are really separating. We have really made it to the place of no return.

It feels all wrong … Then again, I don't know of

any couple who gets married with the intention of splitting up.

Not long after we start packing, we are finished, knowing Ruben will be back for more things at a different time yet having enough to get by for now.

At the front door, I don't know what to do or say.

Stepping out onto the porch, Ruben turns and looks at me. "I never meant for this to hurt you."

Sighing, I whisper, "I don't know of anyone who has been together as long as we have whoever did anything with the intention of hurting their partner. It just happens. We'll get through this." I force a smile. "A bump in the road."

I see the pain in his eyes, and I find satisfaction in the fact that he is hurting, too.

Before he makes it to the end of the porch, I step back then shut and lock the door. Leaning against the doorframe, I wonder if anything will ever feel right again.

How can I find it in myself to trust in anything again? I believed in us. I believed in forever and happily ever after. In less time than it took to build my marriage, it was broken, and I'm left to pick up the pieces. I guess this is step one.

With that in mind, I take the first physical step to my bedroom. One, two, three, four, five … One foot in front of the other, I will keep going.

Lying in bed, I count the tasks to be done tomorrow. One, I will wake up and face a new day. Two, I will get my kids up and ready for school. Three, I will pack my lunch and go to work, a job I am more grateful for by the minute. Without my job, I would have even more to worry about with my marriage falling apart. Four, I will make a budget to ensure I can provide for me and the kids without relying on Ruben.

He's a good provider, but everything is changing between us. I can't guarantee his support for myself or my children. They didn't ask to be born, and they didn't ask for us to separate, so I'm going to bust my butt to make sure they feel the effects of this as little as possible.

Continuing my mental bullet points of tasks, I decide I need to come up with what to tell the kids concerning our situation. At some point, I will need to reach out to Ruben to determine if he plans to eat dinner and go on with nighttime routines with us for a while or just for tomorrow. If he's going to eat here, I need to plan meals accordingly, which will, in turn, cause me to have to adjust my budget for having another mouth to feed.

My mind goes over the many things I need to get done until I finally drift into a restless sleep. When day breaks, I get up before my alarm, needing to give myself time to face the day alone before having the responsibility of motherhood weighing me down further.

I can do this. Day one of finding and remaking myself is here.

With that in mind, I step out of my room and into the kitchen. As if nothing has changed, I make my children breakfast. Today, they get oatmeal. It's certainly not their favorite, but I have a long day with a lot to get done; therefore, I need something easy this morning.

Luckily for me, they are used to Ruben keeping strange hours with the runs, so when he isn't around this morning, they don't ask me any questions. I don't know what to tell them yet. I can't even bring myself to say the D-word.

Will we really get divorced? I have more questions than answers, and I'm pretty sure even Ruby doesn't know. At least I have this break, and tonight, Ruben can help me tackle our explanation.

This morning, I will be thankful for small miracles.

———

After a semi-normal day at work, I am home and trying to sort my mind for dinner. I change into my house clothes of an old T-shirt and lounge pants. Then, walking into the kitchen, I breathe. My sanctuary.

I love to cook. I love being in the kitchen. I love preparing a hot meal for my family.

Family.

What does that mean now?

Moving around, I gather things to make Mexican rice and chicken for dinner. Dicing the onion, I feel like I am cutting my heart, and I fight back the tears that aren't caused by my task at hand.

I have to tell my children that everything they have found security in, everything *we* have found security in is gone. How can I rebuild for them?

The steady tick of the Harley pulling up in our driveway spikes my anxiety even higher. Ruben then makes his way inside while my children don't hide their excitement of seeing their father.

Continuing to focus on dinner, I try to find the words in my head to be able to explain this to my kids, but I draw a blank. How can I help them make sense of something I have yet to figure out?

When Ruben comes to me and places his arm around my hip like he has so many times before, I want to vomit. Fighting my emotions, I shake my head at him.

"It's gonna be okay, Jenna," he whispers into my ear. "I didn't mean for it to be this way."

I choke back a sob. What does he want me to say?

I continue to shake my head. I need him not to touch

me. I need him not to try to take this back. *He* did this to us. He can't kill me figuratively then think it's all going to be okay somehow. Magic like that doesn't exist.

"I'll handle this at dinner," he adds, releasing me.

I don't speak. I simply blow out a heavy breath and finish cooking.

I feel helpless. I feel out of control. The only thing I can do is make our dinner, so I'll focus on making it a good one.

Sitting down at the table we have shared so many meals at, a somberness hits me. This is it.

"Did you have to work early today, Papi?" Mariella asks Ruben, opening the door to the conversation that needs to begin yet I would give anything to avoid.

Ruben lays his fork on his plate, moving his elbows onto the table and lacing his fingers together as if he were saying a prayer. After a moment, he looks up at our daughter. "I stayed at the compound last night."

And so it begins.

"Why?" RJ immediately asks.

As Ruben looks at our children, I can see the pain in his eyes and again find some satisfaction in it. I shouldn't, but I do.

"Sometimes people"—he pauses—"grow apart. Things change."

"Are you and Mami getting a divorce?" Maritza spits out.

I can't help looking at my daughter in shock. "How do you know about divorce?"

They say kids are resilient, but I don't see how they can bounce back from their family falling apart. As a result, the way she calmly answers scares me.

"At school, Jimmy's parents are getting a divorce. He said his dad moved out, and that's how he knows."

"It happens all the time," Mariella adds as if we are discussing a change in vacation, not our entire lives.

Looking at my son, my world crashes once again. Tears are falling from his eyes one by one.

"We won't see you anymore," RJ starts before his emotions become too much.

"No, no, I'll be here. You'll see me every day. I just won't live here. Your mom and I, we just need some space to regroup."

At that answer, RJ wipes his eyes with the back of his hands. Satisfied that they will see their father, the kids seem to take the rest of the night in stride. I'm glad they can, because in my mind, everything is still falling … falling apart.

CHAPTER TEN

NEW ROUTINE

RUBY

ONE MONTH LATER

The duplexes are nice. I have a furnished place to stay. I can't really complain … Only, it definitely isn't home. If I were a single man, I could see living here and being completely satisfied. I'm not a single man, yet in some ways, I am.

What a mess of things I have made. Part of me wants to go out and live the life of a bachelor. I want the rush of no responsibility, the freedom of doing what I want, when I want. The thing is, as much as I think I want that, I can't stop thinking about my wife and children. I can't stop wondering if Jenna is sleeping, if the kids are fighting, or if they need me and I'm not there.

On one hand, I am single and alone. Except, I have dinner every night with my wife and my kids. I leave then come back here to feel the emptiness, all knowing they are at home, full of noise and life, a life I helped build and am walking away from.

We have spent a month creating our new normal. Will anything ever feel right again?

Picking up my phone, I do something I haven't done in so long I can't remember the last time.

"Ruben," she answers on the third ring, "I'm getting the kids ready for school."

"Wanna go out to breakfast together before work?"

I hear her shuffling around, but I get no reply. Faintly, I can make out the sound of a door shutting, I think.

"Ruben, I don't see why we need to be together unless the children are involved."

She was moving to a room where the kids couldn't hear us.

Rubbing my chest, I try to calm the physical pain I feel from her words. "I was thinking—"

"No, don't go there," she interrupts me. "You're

lonely. Nothing has changed with how you feel about me. As the mother of your children, I have an obligation to you where they are concerned. Beyond co-parenting, we don't need to play games with each other. I will not be a doormat. I will not be with a man who doesn't love me for me."

I hate hearing the pain in her voice, pain I caused.

"Jenna, baby, breathe." I sigh. "That wasn't my intention. I just thought—"

"Don't think. I've gotta get the kids on the bus and then get to work. I'll see you tonight for dinner since you set the kids up to expect that. Beyond our children, though, we have nothing to discuss."

The silence that finds me on the other end lets me know she disconnected, and I think on what she said.

I am messing up at every turn. I did make it so the kids expect me at dinner. I didn't think about her. My only thought was how I want my kids to see me every day. I want them to be impacted as little as possible while Jenna and I sort out our issues.

It's not that I don't love her. Can't she see I just miss the person she was before? The passion between us died somewhere over the years. Since everything is about the kids for her, I thought, by making their needs my priority, it wouldn't hurt anything … Although, it somehow did.

Two hours later, my day is not improving, my

thoughts stay on Jenna and how much I fucked everything up. Now I'm in the truck with Frisco, going to get parts for a bike, when we drive by the office for the mini storage.

Jenna is standing outside with some guy I have never seen before, pointing to the storage buildings. She is doing her job and most likely giving him directions. When she looks up, though, I see her smile for the first time since I created this mess for us both.

It's time I really sort myself out so she can do her own thing, too.

"What's up with you, brother?" Frisco asks after we get the parts and get back in the truck.

I shake my head. "You and Tilly"—I bring up his ex, not sure if this will really help me or not—"when did you decide it was done?"

He looks over to me from the driver seat. "Fuck, that bad?"

"That song, you know the one about losing that loving feeling from back in the day?"

Frisco laughs. "Yeah, man, but that's not you and Vida."

"The heat, it's gone."

"Me and Tilly, we were fire and ice. She couldn't handle the life. She felt like the club was more important than her. Every event, every run, damn near every day was a battle in my own home. If I left, I didn't love her, even if I was coming home to her. If I put my cut on one more time, I didn't love her. Hell, if I took a shit that stank, I didn't love her, because I wasn't thinking of her precious fucking nose."

I laugh. "I bet it kept things alive."

"Alive and exhausting. There was never a moment of calm. Back then, things were full of chaos for the club. We were trying to sort out exactly how far over the line of law abiding and outlawing we were willing to go. I had trouble at work, we had trouble in the club, and I damn sure had trouble at home." He makes the right turn back out onto the highway. "I had no escape."

I can understand where the man was coming from.

"It was war between your woman and your club."

"A war she declared unnecessarily. You've got good with Vida, Ruby. She's your escape when the days are long and the runs even longer."

I let out a huff. "When the kids aren't on her brain."

"Brother, she's a mother. She carried them babies inside her body. She felt them long before anyone else could. She held them first. They will always be on her mind. I heard a saying once: men's brains are like waffles. We put everything in a box. If we are in the kid box, then we think of our kids and focus on those needs specifically. When we're fucking our woman, we're fucking our woman. On the flip side of that, women's brains are like spaghetti; everything swirls together. So when they're in the kid zone, they're also thinking of work, home, and their man. A woman can be riding you like she can't get enough of your cock, and in her mind, she could be making a damn grocery list."

"Fuck you, Frisco!" I laugh. "Ain't no one riding my cock and thinking of a grocery list. I work it better than that, brother."

He smirks at me. "So you think."

We both laugh. However, his words hit home. He's right; Jenna's brain is always going. Maybe she got lost in her lack of an escape. When does she get to turn it all off and worry about herself and only herself?

Jenna

G etting home, I am just as irritated with Ruben as I was this morning. How dare he think he can call me up for breakfast like we are old friends! He told me to my face he wasn't in love with me anymore. Sure, I asked the question, and some may view it as I brought this on myself, but never in a million years did I really think he would hesitate and, beyond that, actually tell me he loved me as the mother of his children yet was no longer in love with me.

There is a level of maturity we both must maintain. We have children together. For them, I will not get ugly, or at least, not in front of them. To call me to go to breakfast, though … The man has balls. The wall has been built between us, and it's so high, even if he reached the heavens, he couldn't get to me again.

As I fold some of his remaining clothes into a box,

the dryer goes off, and I move to get the clothes out and add them to the rest. I should have mixed the dirty with the clean and left him to sort it out. I shouldn't have worried over his clothes at all. It's done now, no more. This is another step closer to getting my life back. I gave him too much for too long.

I could not fathom ever being anything other than in love, head over heels in love, seeing fireworks at every touch in love with Ruben Castillo … until now. There is so much anger inside me I don't feel the love. No, I feel the need to move on. I have my kids, and for that alone, I don't wish him any harm. The time for me to find out who I am without Ruben Castillo is here.

I look around our bedroom. I have taken the time to remove our couple pictures. The only ones left are family ones. As much as part of me wants to hate him for the hurt I feel, I can't deny he is still the father of my children, and for life, we will be a family, even if it is a new definition of what we once were.

There was a watch on his dresser, but I dropped it into the top drawer. Visibly, I have cleared him from our marital space as much as possible.

Going into my bathroom, I look into the mirror.

"I am strong." Thinking of my childhood, I sigh. "I have been through worse. Besides, I have my babies." I blow out a breath. "I am a damn good mother," I say with all the confidence in the world. I may not have done anything else right in my life, but I am a damn good mom. "I am beautiful … in my children's eyes."

Rolling my shoulders back, I gather my strength. "No more tears allowed. I am Jenna Mariella Natera de Castillo, and I will survive this."

Pep talk complete, I go to the kitchen and set the table. Ruben arrives not long after the pizza I ordered does, and like every other night since our separation, we sit down and eat. The casual pleasantries commence, and our children share their day as if nothing has changed when, in essence, everything has fallen apart.

He tucks the kids in for bed while I move the box to the front porch and wait outside. When he finds me, he laughs, making fire build inside me like never before.

"Oh, my stuff goes outside once again, Vida. Why not in the yard?"

I glare. "No, your stuff goes in my van for me to return to you tomorrow after work."

"Is that so?"

"You fucked up my life, Ruben!" I yell, praying that, since we are outside, my children can't hear. I need this, though. I need to get it out. "You fucked up our life. Everything we built, you made crumble."

"Oh, now she has fire," he goads.

"Don't push me too far. You created this mess, and now you come and go like it's nothing. I'm over here, doing your laundry. That ends today. I'm cooking your meals? Tonight was your last one. If you wanna see the kids, fine, but you don't get to eat meals with us. You can take them out on Wednesday nights. You can have every other weekend, like normal, separated parents do."

As he steps into my space, I inhale his scent, and my heart beats even faster.

"You want papers; is that where this is headed, Vida? It's been a month. We're still sorting shit."

"I'm your Vida no more. I'm not your life. Your life is your own. As for papers, let me make one thing clear to you, Ruben Castillo."

"Yeah?" He smirks, getting off on my anger. "What's that?"

"I'm not signing shit! I was the first Mrs. Ruben Castillo, and I'll be the only. I'll be damned if all the years building this life together end with some barfly raising my kids and having their name. You're gonna give me that, too, out of respect for our children."

"Is that so?" He smiles. "I see my wife found her heat again."

"There is nothing about this you should be smiling about. As for my heat, you should be careful. I'm not sure you can take the flame."

"Oh, baby, I can more than handle the flame. I just don't ever want to see it fizzle again." He kisses my forehead quickly. "This is the woman I fell in love with.

This is the woman I breathe for." He watches me as he backs off the porch, still smirking. "See you tomorrow, Vida."

"Fuck you, Ruben Castillo, and the steel horse you rode here on."

CHAPTER ELEVEN

FAMILY REDEFINED

RUBY

SIX MONTHS LATER

The Hellions annual barbeque is here. All the chapters, charters, affiliates, and families are at the thirty-acre compound. Business is off the table today. This is an event for appreciation and family coming together.

Helping to line up the pig cooker and the other

barrel grills for hotdogs and hamburgers, I am caught off guard when Roundman approaches my side.

"Ruby, is Vida coming out today?"

Placing the bricks under the tires to keep them from rolling, I then look at the president of my club.

The man has aged well. His long hair is braided down his back, and his goatee is trimmed with streaks of gray. He is tall and built like he works out at a gym regularly, even though he doesn't. He is a man I look up to, not only for his role within the club, but because he's the type of man who truly leads by example. He is the walking, talking real deal of what he expects every man around him to be. He has been more of a father to me than the man who created me.

"Yeah," I reply, moving to block up the next grill.

"That doesn't sound too sure."

I swear the man can read minds sometimes. I pause, putting my hands on my hips and looking to the ground. I don't know how Roundman feels about my separation. Is he disappointed in me? We haven't had any time to really talk about it.

"It's my weekend with the kids, so she'll at least be here to drop them off. Hopefully, having Doll here, she'll want to stay and hang out with the girls."

He rubs his goatee in thought. "I get things aren't good with you two. Typically, when an ol' lady and her man split"—he pauses—"well, I hate to say it, but typically, the club splits, too."

I raise an eyebrow at him in question, not following.

"We are a brotherhood first. A lot of times, if things go south, we ride with our brother."

Not being someone who is good at reading between the lines, I ask, "What are you trying to tell me?"

He looks at me as if he's trying to get the words right, and for the first time, I wonder about my position in the club.

"Can't leave her out, brother."

Apprehension fills me. "I never expected you to."

He can't really think I would want the club to turn their backs on Jenna. She's here because of me. She left everything and everyone behind to be here with Julio and me. When her brother got in trouble, she could have gone back to Mexico, but she didn't. She stayed and chose to ride it out with me.

"I hate watching both of you go through this. I know you've got your reasons. I've been around a long time, Ruby. I had a love like yours once. Lost it to fucking cancer. I get you've got shit to work on, but you've got time and you've got opportunity. Instead of hoping the girls keep your ol' lady hanging around, why don't you be the reason she stays?"

Before I can reply, he slaps me in the man way on the shoulder and walks away.

Could I find a way to be the reason she stays? Over the last few months, she has gone out with Pami and Sass a few times. She has found a new routine. She dresses up, gets her nails done, wears makeup when she's going out, and she even went and had her hair cut and styled.

Our interactions have been kept to the kids. I have tried to talk to her as a friend. I have tried to have something more between us than our children. However, the more fire she finds back in herself, the more she pushes me away.

Making my way around front, I watch her van pull into the compound. My kids jump out as soon as she opens the door. All three run to me for hugs I gladly give before sending them on their way inside. I don't have to worry over them here. There are enough ol' ladies around to make sure they are having fun and not killing each other so I can try to convince my wife to stay for a little while.

"Jenna," I greet, shutting her car door behind her.

"Ruben," she replies, attempting to walk away as I reach out and squeeze her arm gently.

"Wait," I start. "Before you go in there, can we have a minute?"

"Ruben, I've been an ol' lady long enough; I know how to act," she says in an exasperated tone. "Whether we're together or not, I still represent you. I get it. No need for the breakdown. I'll follow the rules and not make you look bad in front of your brothers."

"I love that heat you're throwing around, Vida."

She throws her hand up at me. "Stop, Ruben."

"I know. I know I'm pushing too far. I did this, and I have to accept it. I just wanted to have a minute to tell you thanks for coming out, and I want you to stay and have a good time today. Regardless of what goes on with me and you, the Hellions are your family, too."

She smiles at me. "Doll already told me the same thing and asked me to not take off early."

I raise my eyebrow at her in silent question.

"I'll hang around for a little while," she says, but the very moment I start to think I have a little bit of hope, she adds, "with the girls."

Without another word, she walks off with a swing to her jean-covered hips I haven't seen in years. Damn, she's hot like fire.

I follow her inside like a lost, damn dog, and I don't even give a shit that I look like a whipped, little puppy. I will be her bitch any day to have back what we lost.

JENNA

Jenna

The last few months have been a hard transition, though a necessary one. I don't believe marriages fall apart on their own. As hard as it is, I have to look inside myself and be accountable for my failures.

It would be easy to sit back and say love is a choice and Ruben made his. It would be easy to sit back and call my girlfriends to whine and bitch. It would be easy to tell the world, "He's an asshole and lost the best thing that ever happened to him," screaming it at the top of my lungs. It would be easy to simply hate him for hurting me.

What would any of that accomplish, though? What would any of that repair? The damage is done.

The fact is, I am not the same woman he fell in love with or married, just as he is not the same man I fell in love with or married. Somehow, over time, I got lost in being married, being a mom, and after that, I added in a full-time job.

Sometimes, saying nothing at all was easier because the truth of the matter was I had no energy left inside me to fight. When I looked in the mirror, I couldn't see anything left of myself except my stamp of motherhood. As magical and wonderful as that is, where does that leave me? Where does that leave Jenna?

The answer is daunting.

It left me depleted. It left me numb. It left me unable to be anything more than the mother of my children. Most days, I went through the motions. I went from one task to the next, surviving. I have learned in this process that existing is not living.

Passion, wants, and desires, they fuel us. Getting by, while there is a season for it in life, is merely that— getting by. And it can be draining in its own way.

Ruben wanted the fire back between us. I failed him. I failed our marriage.

What I didn't do was do it alone. Ruben failed us, too. He could have worked to keep the spark alive. He could have refused to accept my complacency. He could have called me out on my descent down the rabbit hole of existence. He didn't.

He let me fall. He let us fail. Rather than find a solution, he fell out of love. He fell out of patience. He turned his back on what we built.

Together, we failed each other. Together, we destroyed what we so carefully created. Together, we failed to protect each other and our union. Together, we have now found a new life apart while respecting each other as the parents to our children.

Putting a little more sway in my step, I make my way inside the compound. The past is the past, and my future is and always will be tied to this club.

The first person I see is Pami, and I quickly give her a hug, feeling Ruben's eyes on my ass the whole time.

Watch all you want, mister. It's not yours anymore. I smile, thinking to myself, *No, I belong to me.* And I finally, for the first time in a long time, love me for me. For the first time since having my first daughter, my validation doesn't come from being a mom or the milestones in my children's lives.

Ruben is right behind me as Boomer comes over to join Pam and me when a barfly makes her way over. I roll my eyes yet keep my composure. If she wants to come over here, so be it.

"Boomer," Ruben greets him in that half-hug thing they do. He is starting to talk when the barfly walks in front of me to him.

Handing him the cold beer in her hand, she smiles.

"Thought you might be thirsty. You've been working hard while setting up, Ruby."

I can't hold back my laugh as she openly hits on my husband in front of me. Pami is glaring at the woman while Boomer watches her, wide-eyed.

"I'm married," Ruben says to her.

"Rumor has it you're living on the compound, and you're separated." She takes a pull of the beer she brought over for him. "I figured we could share a drink and relax a little."

"Taken," Ruben confirms once more, this time lifting his tattooed ring finger up for evidence.

I laugh harder. "Rumor is true. Don't let him fool you, sweetheart. He's just not interested in you. He lives on the compound, and he's no longer taken. You can have him all you want, but I warn you now, stay the fuck away from my kids." I lower my voice. "If you even say hello to my children, I'll cut you, bitch. Know that."

She chokes on the beer, looking at me like I'm crazy. She should know, if she fucks with my kids, I *am* bat-shit fucking crazy.

Ruben looks from her to me, then me to her before back to me. "I'm not taken, huh? Who's not signing shit, Vida?"

Oh, that's the game he wants to play.

I put my hand on my hip and look him dead in his eyes, "*I'm* not signing shit, mother fucker; that's who."

The barfly, not knowing what to do, moves away. "Apparently, you two have some stuff to work out. I'll see you around, Ruby."

"Don't bother," he barks back before looking at me. "Can't have it both ways, Vida. Can't keep me and turn me loose."

"I'm not trying to have you. I'm keeping a name for my kids."

He smiles and steps closer to me. "Keep telling yourself it's for your kids. Truth is, baby, it's yours. There will only ever be one Mrs. Ruben Castillo, and she's right in front of my face."

"Ruben, we're done playing games with each other," I say firmly.

"No games, baby. I fucked up. I lost you because I didn't hold on tightly enough. I lost us to life, work, kids, and everything in between. That's on me, Vida. I know what I had, what I lost, and I damn sure will fight to get it back."

"There's nothing to get back."

He laughs as he leans in and whispers, "The lies we tell ourselves don't change the truth. Don't fight us; never fight us. Fight *for* us, Vida, not against us."

CHAPTER
TWELVE

FIGHT FOR US

RUBY

I have had my moment, my epiphany. I fucked up, but in the process, my woman found herself again.

I'm hot for her. I'm hot for us. The heat is back and stronger than ever. For the first time in I can't remember when, I feel again. I feel alive.

Life. Vida.

Things aren't right yet, but they will be. I will fight until the end to have my family back.

Two days after the barbeque, I'm at work with my mind on my family. Going into the office, I pull out my wallet.

"Amy," I greet our receptionist, "I need to order some flowers for my wife to be delivered to her work. Sign the card from my kids."

Amy's eyes get big. "Roses or anything particular?"

"Something bright to make her smile." I toss my credit card on her desk.

"Someone got his head outta his ass," Frisco says, coming in the office from behind me.

I laugh yet don't argue with him.

I have had opportunities to be with other women, but they aren't my wife. They aren't Jenna. They don't spark inside me what she does. They don't have the loyalty she does.

Having this time, these nights alone in my duplex without my kids, without her laying over me, I realize just how good I had it.

If you love something, set it free … I will never be free, nor do I want to be. We are tied together by our children, but more than that, by our connection to each other.

"Thanks for helping me, Amy," I say, exiting the room and going back to work.

Frisco joins me not long after. He has tasked himself with taking care of Amy since the Delatorre situation that landed Tank in the hospital so long ago. She's finally not the skittish mouse she was when she first arrived, and I can't help wondering if she can be the Hellions original's chance at love—real love and real loyalty.

"I'm proud of you, Ruby."

"For what?"

"Figuring your shit out before it got too late and too much time was lost. The thing about life is it passes in the blink of an eye. Long before we realize it, we lose time, too much time. There are a few things you can't get back, and that's one of them."

I look at him over the hood of the Camaro we are working on. "You speak the truth, brother."

He smirks. "Always. Next time, you should listen sooner."

"There won't be a next time. I'm not letting go again."

"Good to know."

We finish work, and I'm putting my tools up for the day when my phone pings with a text.

Nice touch. Thank you for the flowers. They made me smile.

Oh, what I wouldn't give to have seen that smile for myself.

Replying, I send up a silent prayer that she will be receptive.

I'm sorry ... for everything. My head is outta my ass now.

Waiting around, I get anxious for a reply. When one doesn't come after a little bit, I figure she's driving and will reply later, so I make my way to my duplex.

I'm just pulling my boots off when my phone rings, and the display has me smiling.

"Vida," I answer.

"I'm driving, so I didn't want to text you back, and I want to have this conversation when the children aren't around."

My heart sinks at her tone. "What conversation is that?"

"You've gotta know, Ruben..." She pauses, and I hear her breathe deeply.

"You got someone else?" I bark out the first thing that comes to mind.

She huffs in exasperation. "No, sonso." I laugh at her calling me names. "You need to know nothing between us changes. You can't wake up one day and decide you love me again, and all is forgiven."

She's right. More than being right, I don't expect nor would I want her to be eager to go straight back to where we were.

"I don't want that, Vida."

"What do you want then?"

"A second chance," I simply say. "A new beginning. We have grown. We both have changed. I want the woman you are to be the woman you are with me. I don't want a doormat, never have. I want to fuck up and have you call me on it. I want us to be together, but you as Jenna, not just as my wife—as your own self."

She's quiet for a beat. "I don't know if I can get passed the hurt."

Damn, I sure have made a mess of things.

"I understand, but I want a chance to make it right. I want a chance for us to find each other again. I want a chance to find the heat between us again."

"I don't even know where to begin to rebuild," she replies honestly and in a somewhat sad tone.

"The same way it all started years ago." I pause, giving her time to think. "Friendship. You have always been more than Julio's little sister; you have always been my friend first."

"And how do you suggest we do that?"

"Dinner. You, me, and if you're more comfortable, the kids," I say with a little too much hope in my voice.

"No kids. I don't want to give them the wrong idea. I don't want them to be caught in some game between us."

"No game."

She sighs. "I wish I could believe it."

I deserve that. It's my fault she has no faith in me, in us. I will spend the rest of my life giving her something to believe in every single day. We both failed to hold on to what we created. I am just as guilty as she is.

"Just give me a chance."

While she remains on the phone, I can hear the sounds of her car running, but she doesn't speak.

"Give *us* a chance," I plead.

"I need time."

"Understood." I pause. "No matter what, Vida, I want you to be happy and secure. I sent the flowers just to put a smile on your face. This has been hard on us both. I was thinking of you and our kids, and I just wanted you to know you're appreciated."

There is no hesitation. "It was a great surprise and much appreciated."

"Be safe getting home, Vida. Give the kids my love."

"Will do. Goodnight, Ruben."

He can't honestly think, because he has suddenly figured out what he wants, I'm going to accept it. Ruben may want me back, but can he handle the person I am? I refuse to get lost after I found myself again. I found Jenna Mariella Natera de Castillo. I can look in the mirror and be proud.

I am strong.

I am loyal.

I am a great damn mom.

I am a hard worker.

I am beautiful … and not just because my kids think it.

I am the best damn thing that ever walked into Ruben Castillo's life.

The flowers today were nice. I was surprised because he's never done that before. To put them from our children was an added bonus.

Can I find a way to work through all the pain? Can we really have a second chance?

It's all too much. I don't know how to process any of this.

My thoughts go crazy as a light on my dashboard catches my attention, and the ping of my gas monitor alerting me to low fuel leaves me exhausted. Can I ever catch a break?

I laugh to myself, thinking of the many times Ruben has gotten so mad at me when he's gotten in the van and it's below a quarter of a tank.

"Vida, don't put yourself in a situation to have to worry about running out."

"Jenna, do you know how bad this is for the engine? Letting it get this low will draw the crud up and junk up your injectors. Now we need to make sure you have a clean fuel filter. Just more work for me."

"If pumping gas is that much of a chore, tell me when you get to a quarter of a tank, and I'll fill it up."

"Every damn time I get in your van, you've got no gas. Do you ever pump gas?"

I can hear him in my head as I mentally figure out how many miles I should have left. I contemplate just filling up in the morning, but then decide against pushing my luck.

Stopping at the next gas station, I pull up to the pump with my mind all over the place then get out without thinking about my surroundings. I don't think about anything except my husband wanting a second chance. I pull the lever by the driver's door to pop open the gas cover. Leaning inside my van, I get my credit card from my purse. I'm sticking it in the pump when I hear my phone ping with a text. Worried it could be about the kids, I go back to the driver's door and reach for my phone.

There is a shadow that moves in, causing me to lean in more as my phone starts to ring. Julio's contact information is the last thing I see before something solid comes down on the back of my head and neck, and then the darkness ensues. Limp.

Out cold.

The last noise I hear is my phone ringing and the gas pump dinging for me to remove my card. My last thought is: why is my brother calling now? We talk on weekends when it's cheaper, so what's the emergency?

If only my mind had been on the alert, maybe I could have realized the emergency was me.

Time is lost.

Desperation hits me as the pain radiates from the back of my head and down my spine. I blink.

Darkness.

My eyelashes feel something soft. Blindfolded … I'm blindfolded.

I start move my hands, only to find my wrists are tied. What the hell is happening?

I was at the gas station. My phone rang … My brother called. Why?

The pain.

Someone has me. Why?

While I don't speak, my breathing is heavy and loud. I bite against the dirty cloth gagging my mouth. If someone is watching me, I need to calm down and get myself together.

Slowly, I try to pull my feet apart, only to find my ankles have also been bound.

Senses. Think, Jenna.

Sight: I blink again. The cloth against my eyes is soft but dark, so I move my gaze down. There is a crack where I can see slightly. However, my surroundings are too dark to make out anything with my limited visibility.

Smell: I breathe in deeply. There are no distinct smells around me.

Taste: The cloth in my mouth is rough and dry. It tastes of dirt and feels like a shop rag Ruben would have out in the garage.

Touch: I twist my hands and struggle to feel behind me and under me. Hard. Metal.

Sound: Sitting quietly, I try to ignore the throbbing in my head enough to listen to everything around me. Silence.

I'm in the dark, some place alone, sitting on metal, like in the back of a work van. I'm not able to move easily, see, or speak. Okay, think, Jenna.

The kids are with Pam and Boomer. When I don't arrive, she will call Ruben.

Time. How long have I been out? Are my kids

worried by now? Does Ruben even know I have been taken? I know Pamela and Boomer will take care of my babies. I just don't know how they will handle me being gone. I have never failed to be where I said I would be for my kids.

Why have I been taken? Is it because of the Hellions?

Certainly, whoever has me knows I'm of no value to the club. Hell, I'm technically not an ol' lady to the Hellions right now.

The club has rules. They have a code they live by. Women are supposed to be off limits. This isn't the first time a woman would have been targeted based on association, though. Doll was watched by Delatorre and put in enough danger that Roundman felt the need to send her away. The club handled business, but lives were lost, and Tank ended up in a coma for quite some time.

In Catawba, there was an issue when a club we were doing business with had a member attack Tessie who was under club protection. Retribution was had, and in the end, Tessie and Shooter found love. Rex, too, found his ol' lady when he had to protect her from situations not related to the club.

This could be anything.

Only, for me, my job, my life, it's all tied to the Hellions. I just have to have faith in the club. I have to believe they will find me before anything worse happens.

As I lean back against the cold metal behind me, I have one nagging thought I can't let go of: why was Julio calling me right before I was taken?

CHAPTER THIRTEEN

13

TORTURED

RUBY

My phone rings while I'm in the shower. When the number comes up as unknown, I don't give it any more thought.

Microwaving a frozen meal, I think about how badly I really have messed up.

We all go through things, bumps in the road of life. Sometimes, we get knocked off course. I took my wife and the life we built together for granted. I was selfish to even think there could be more out there when what we had was good. As the old saying goes, *if it ain't broke, don't fix it.* Why didn't I follow the mantra? Why did I go borrowing trouble?

Suddenly, there is a pounding on my front door.

"Hold the hell on. Damn," I yell as I set down the slop I was going to choke down for dinner and make my way to the entrance. Opening the door, I am in no way prepared for Roundman, Frisco, Danza, Tank and the local police.

I throw my hands up in the air. "I've got papers. Dammit, Roundman, tell them I've got papers!"

My first thought is Jenna. Is this some immigration thing? Is she okay? We are legit. Roundman helped us with it. Our kids are legal. Why is there a cop coming into my place?

Frisco squeezes my shoulder. "We're not here for that, Ruby."

"I think you should sit down, brother," Tank adds, moving in behind me.

Adrenaline pumps through my veins. "What the ever-loving fuck are you here for?"

The cop steps forward. "Are you Ruben Castillo?"

"Si," I answer in Spanish as my mind races at warp speed. "Yes. I mean, yes."

"Is your wife Jenna Castillo?"

"Yes, she is my wife, my life. Why are you asking about Vida?"

His next question floors me. "Are you estranged?"

My world stops. I feel like I have been punched in the gut. I can't breathe, can't stand, can't move. Somehow, I nod my head as I feel Tank wrap an arm around my shoulders, keeping me upright.

"When was the last time you spoke to your wife?"

"To-to-tonight … when she got off from work. Where is my wife?"

"There was an incident at the Handy Mart tonight," the cop begins, and I lunge forward, wrapping my hands around his throat.

"What do you mean an incident? Where the fuck is my wife?" I release him harshly and begin to pace. I look to Roundman. "My kids, who has them?"

"Calm down, brother," Roundman orders. "Your kids are with Pam and Boomer and don't know anything."

I look to the man who is a father figure to me. "Where is Vida?"

Roundman looks to the cop to continue.

"Your wife was attacked."

At his words, I fall to the floor. The room spins, and rage fills me.

"I'll kill the son of a bitch who touches one hair on her. I'll fucking gut them."

Two, firm hands come down on my shoulders, squeezing. Tank is trying to keep me in place as the cop continues.

"Sir, please refrain from threats. I understand your emotions; however, as an officer of the law, I have to take those seriously, regardless of your place within the Hellions Motorcycle Club."

I glare.

"At approximately 1830 tonight, a Honda Odyssey minivan registered to you was taped on a security camera pulling up to pump seven. Your wife is seen putting her card in the pump and then moving back to her driver's seat. At this time, we are unsure the reason she did not continue with her purchase. A person covered in dark clothing and wearing a mask is then taped hitting your wife over the head with a blunt object."

I shudder and fight the urge to tear everything up in my path.

"The clerk then hit the silent alarm as she watched the person lift your wife's limp body and carry it over to an eighties model, full-size, black, Chevy van with no plates. Once your wife was inside the van, the driver, who was a different masked individual, pulled away."

Fear turns like a cyclone in my stomach. Someone has my wife. Someone hit my wife over the head and took her. All of the unknowns scare me.

Is she okay? Have they harmed her more? What are they doing to her?

Unable to keep myself contained, I jump up and rush to the bathroom where I vomit until I am left dry heaving over the toilet. Then, looking over my shoulder at Roundman, I feel helpless.

"Please tell me this is not blowback on the club."

He shakes his head. "From what we have gathered, no. I can't make you any promises about why she was taken, but I can tell you this: we will do everything we can to bring her home and seek retribution for touching what belongs to our club. She's family, and she's off limits. Someone crossed a line, and they will pay for it. And pay dearly."

I take a moment to compose myself—it's my time to be strong for my wife and children. Then, stepping into my living room, I sit down with the officer and my club brothers.

My torture begins. As time passes by, I answer question after question. All the while, my mind races with thoughts of what is happening to Jenna. My whole body is in pain, needing to know she's okay, yet I'm stuck in place with not even the first lead as to who took her or where they have her.

This kind of torture would have me giving up any government secrets I ever knew just to have the knowledge of her wellbeing.

After finishing the questions, the officer and his partner, who had stayed silent in the corner the whole time, left me alone with my Hellions brothers.

"The boys in blue are out. Now tell me what happened to Vida."

Frisco is the first to answer, "Really, brother, there isn't blowback on the club that we can find."

"Fuck!" I roar.

My phone starts ringing again, and I look to the screen.

Unknown number.

"Hello," I clip into the phone.

"Llamale a Julio," a Latino voice instructs before disconnecting the call.

More questions and no answers. All of this is torture to me.

JENNA

Jenna

My head is still pounding as time passes by. I don't know where I am or how long I have been here. I fight not to pass out again.

As I twist my wrists, they burn against the rope holding them together. My stomach rolls, and the need to pee hits me full-on, making me groan in agony.

Silence continues to fill the space around me.

Alone.

I am completely alone.

Insanity sets in as I let my mind go crazy with thoughts.

Will I get to see the beautiful brown eyes of my baby girls again? Will I get the chance to fight with little RJ's hair in the morning before school? Where are they? Did the same people get them, as well? I tell myself over and over again my children are okay. I left them with Boomer and Pam, who would die before they let anything happen to my babies. Still, my chest aches with longing and worry for them.

Then my mind goes to my husband. Ruben wants to make it right between us. Will we be given the opportunity? Will I ever see him again?

Love is the most passion-fueled emotion we feel. It hurts the most, cuts the deepest, and leaves the ugliest scars. On the flip side of the coin, it has the ability to make us feel whole. Finding love heals our insecurities.

Love is a verb. It is an action. It takes thought and work.

Love is a noun. When you call someone your love, they become the personification of that thing.

Love is an adjective. It describes how we feel.

I love Ruben, mi amor. I am who I am today because of him and the depth of my emotions for him. When it all falls apart, we must go back to where it was from the start.

Simplify.

Once, there was a boy and a girl. They were faced with the struggles of a life full of danger and poverty. They beat the odds … together. They built a solid life for themselves and their children.

Ruben and I have come from nothing. We may not have a mansion in Beverly Hills, but we do have love. We lost sight of this. In the changes of life, in the hurt from words, and in the whirlwind of many emotions, we lost sight of where it all began: one boy, one girl, one love for one life.

I bite against my gag as tears fall down my face. Will I die not being able to tell him I forgive him? Will I die without one last touch of his lips against mine? Will I die here in this van or container alone?

The salt in the air off the ocean breeze calms me. Today is the day Ruben and I will say our vows before God, Julio, and a few people we have made friends with on the farm. Sure, we did things a little unconventionally by living together before we were a couple. Then we had Maritza before we got married.

We weren't legal citizens, though. We couldn't simply go to the court house and get a marriage license without raising some sort of suspicion.

With all the things we weren't, the one thing we have always been is in love—head over heels, top to toe in love.

Julio has been the most supportive of our relationship. He says he finds comfort in Ruben being able to take care of me if something were to happen to him. Again, my brother is looking out for me and my long-term wellbeing.

Ruben is prospecting for the Hellions Motorcycle Club. The guy we stopped to help on the side of the road back when I was pregnant turned out to be one hell of a guy. He has helped both of us secure our citizenship documents. He paid for it out of the club's money. It wasn't until we were right by the law that he would let Ruben prospect.

I don't know if club life is for us. Roundman says, if not, we still don't owe him a thing. It is hard to believe, but what other options do we have? He knows too much.

We found a little Hispanic chapel on the beach, and the priest agreed to marry us as he understood our previous predicament. Today, I get to stand on the coast of North Carolina and pledge my unwavering love to my husband.

Thinking back to the day we got married, I know my love for Ruben has never wavered. Sure, it has changed. I love him in different ways than I did back then. The innocence of our youth has long since passed. Our relationship has settled and matured. Is that what spiraled Ruben out of love? All the changes?

Will I ever get a chance to sort out our marriage? Will I ever get to stand on the beach, hand in hand, with my husband again? Fear grips me as I struggle against my bindings once again.

Fighting back the anxiety of the unknown, I get angry. I can't give up. Ruben and the Hellions will find me. Hell hath no fury like a Hellion when lines are crossed.

Family is off limits!

I don't know who took me or why, but none of that matters. I'm Ruben 'Ruby' Castillo's wife. Ride or die, we're motherfucking Hellions.

I smile against my gag. Watch out, assholes; the whole club is coming for you.

I laugh to myself. One thing I know is Roundman and the club won't stand for this. They will find me.

I just have to hope it's not too late when they do.

HOLDING ON

RUBY

B efore I can wrap my head around anything, my phone rings again. The display shows my brother-in-law calling, and I can't help the dread that creeps up inside me.

"Hermano," I answer.

"Jenna with you?" he immediately barks into the phone.

"No, she's been taken."

Before I can get another word out, he is going off. "I'm gonna fucking gut them. When I get done, their own mothers won't recognize their ugly mugs. No one fuckin' touches mi hermana."

As I look at my Hellions' brothers in the room with me, my temper is boiling. "You need to talk, amigo, and now!" I roar.

"I'll handle it. Keep the kids safe."

The click of the phone disconnecting has me seeing red.

"Julio!" I yell.

No reply.

I start to throw my phone, but Danza's firm hand grips my wrist.

Motherfucking shit. This whole situation went from bad to worse.

He takes the phone out of my hand. "Gotta keep the lines of communication open, brother," Danza says, reminding me to keep my head clear. If I break the phone, how can Vida reach out?

I look to Roundman. "Get Boomer and Pam with the kids and Pam's mom to the compound and locked down."

"The whole club need to be locked in?" Frisco asks, already pulling out his phone to handle business.

I shake my head and stand up to pace the living

room. "I don't think so. I think my family is the only target."

"Why you?" Roundman asks the question I know they are all silently asking.

I have one answer: "Julio Natera."

Tank and Frisco speak at the same time. "Jenna's brother in Mexico?"

I nod my head, wanting to scream, throw something, or punch someone. Guilt fills me. I should have kept a better watch on him. Sure, we send money home, but idle minds have a way of finding trouble, especially when that's all he knows. With everything going on with Jenna and our relationship, I haven't even thought to check up on what her brother has been up to.

"Julio, what the fuck have you done?" I yell.

"You can't lose your cool now!" Danza commands. "We have more information than we started with. That's a step in the right direction."

Danza nods to Frisco who looks to Roundman. When the club president gives a nod, Frisco stands and goes to my front door.

"Where the hell are you going?" I ask, feeling helpless.

Frisco smirks. "To handle business."

I am ready to snap. "Gotta keep me in the loop here."

"You're barely holdin' on, brother," Tank points out. "Let the club handle business for you."

I retort, "This is Mexican shit—"

"Got a guy who knows a guy who knows another guy, type of shit, Ruby. Let us handle this," Danza says.

Can I do this? Can I sit back and rely on my brothers to handle business while my wife is missing?

Fuck no.

I rush to the door, but before I can reach it, Frisco, Roundman, and Danza are holding me back.

"We'll share any information with you," Danza explains. "We've gotta make some calls and use some markers, brother. You've gotta chill and show your kids everything is going to be all right."

"When we find them, I'm gonna kill every mother-fucker who touched her, slowly and painfully."

Roundman looks me right in my eyes. "We'll make sure you get that opportunity, brother. You have my word."

My mind goes back to the vows I gave my wife years ago.

I have no nerves. People say they are nervous on their wedding day. I am not. I am confident in what I have with Jenna and what we will build in the future. Jenna has always and will always be my other half. Today, two become one, as they say, and instead of having nerves, I am filled with pride.

Since losing my mother, no one has been as close to me as Jenna. She is the light in my every moment. She is my reason for waking up and working so hard. She has been my reason even before we got together.

The weather is perfect: not too hot, not too cold. The humidity isn't sticky, and the gentle wind is soothing while I stand at the altar and pledge my vows without hesitation.

"Today, I give you my word to stand by your side through sickness and in health, through good times and bad. In word and in deed, I will love you for the past, for the now, and for the future."

The ocean breeze blows, and her ivory sundress whips around her legs as her eyes stay focused on mine. Here we are, hand in hand, in front of God, our priest, our friends, and our little family, pledging ourselves to each other forever.

I remember that day like it was yesterday. I had it all. In that moment, I knew I had found my forever. Then I lost it. I lost my head. I lost my focus. I lost my love. I'm barely holding on, but in this moment, I promise myself and my wife, when I get her back, we will never be apart again.

Day in and day out with the same person, there are far too many things I took for granted. If I wanted the heat to stay alive in our marriage, I needed to work for it as hard as I expected my wife to. We were two individuals who made a decision to become one unit. That takes two individuals working together toward the same goal. Over time, needs change, but we have to change together.

I let that slip away. I let us fail. I let my wife down when I allowed myself to lose my feelings. I made the choice to let it all slip through my fingers.

Now I know. Now I fight. Once I find her, I will spend my last breath giving her back everything she's given me—life. I don't care what it takes. I will show her in word and deed that I do not only love her, but I'm *in* love with her for the woman she was, is, and will become.

I am not giving up on her. I am not giving up on us. I damn sure am not giving up on our family.

I am barely holding on when the noise of metal sliding on metal sounds in front of me.

"Jenna Natera," a man's voice calls out. "Hola, hermana."

That voice is not Julio. Why is he calling me *sister*?

I shake my head back and forth. I can't see. I can't fight. Am I back in Mexico?

"Llevarla," the voice commands as two arms pull me to them and toss me over someone's shoulder.

The need to pee is too much with the pressure from my new angle, so I let loose all over myself and my captor.

"Carajo," the man carrying me cries out.

"I've given birth to three kids, shithead," I mutter behind my gag, so it comes out sounding like the teacher on a Charlie Brown cartoon.

Deciding I have a small opportunity, I start wiggling. All the twisting makes it hard for him to hold me, so he drops me, and I hit the pavement hard, crying out in agony as pain shoots through my entire body. I will not be deterred, though.

I continue to lash around, wiggling like a worm. Not being able to see where people are, I'm wasting precious energy. I'm barely holding on, but I need to feel like I'm doing something. I will fight until I can't fight anymore.

"Stop!" a man's voice orders.

I don't obey.

Cold metal is pressed against my head and I still. I

know without seeing there is a gun resting on my temple.

"Get her inside," the same voice commands, and once again, I am scooped up and thrown over someone's shoulder.

My mind races. I still don't know how long I was knocked out from the gas station. I don't know how long I spent alone after that. I don't know what day it is. More so, I don't know if I'm still in North Carolina. Hell, I don't even know if I'm still in the United States.

Once inside, I'm tossed to a hard chair. I can sense two men, one on each side of me. My wrists are cut free yet immediately grabbed from either side and tied to the back of the chair. My shoulders burn from the awkward angle, just as they cut my ankles free and tie them to each front leg of the chair.

It takes two grown men to handle me, I think to myself. *Well, they damn sure better be ready when the Hellions come.*

"Your brother has made many enemies on his rise." The voice sounds like the man is on my left.

My brother … What does Julio have to do with anything? His rise to what?

The feel of cold metal tracing my neck puts me on edge. Biting hard on my gag, I try to ignore the blade of the knife tickling my skin in warning.

"The thing is, we can do whatever we want to you,

and your older brother can't get here in enough time to save you."

The weight of the blade pressing down causes me to hold my breath. The knife pierces my skin, and blood trickles down my neck, but I can tell it's not deep.

This is a warning.

"Take the pic. Send it to Natera."

I swallow my fear. I refuse to cry in front of these men. I will not give them any more power over me than they already have. I drop my head.

It's time to endure.

I close my eyes and let my mind be free.

The sensation of the wind against my arms is exhilarating.

I scoot closer to Ruben, my legs wrapped around him as he drives.

The Sportster is small. Its purpose is to teach Ruby to ride. The single seat left no room for me. However, this won't stop me from riding with my man.

I climbed behind him proudly. Wrapping my legs around him, my calves rested against the gas tank as I secured myself Indian-style around my man.

Holding tight, I lean into him as we go down the open road.

"Ride with me, Vida. Ride with me for life," Ruben calls out as he twists the throttle, pushing us to go faster.

I squeeze him. "Always, Ruby. Me and you, always."

Oh, how I wish we were on that bike right now, on the open road. Instead, I'm in a room, tied to a chair, helpless as the man beside me cuts my clothes away.

Shame fills me as I am left naked in this chair within a room filled with I don't know how many.

Silently, I send up a prayer that Ruben will come soon. *Please don't let them violate me.*

The blade is sharp against my collarbone as he cuts me once more. I inhale sharply. It burns, but it's not deep. I can't help feeling like a pawn in a game I don't know the rules to. I wish my brother were here to explain why this is even happening.

The blade starts at my temple under the blindfold, the burn moving down my face as it separates my skin. My cheek is on fire as the knife is then placed against my shoulder. Twisting and driving in, he continues to twirl the tip into my body. Deeper and deeper, it goes.

I bite against my gag and fight back tears. The burn, the pain, the emotions, and being stuck have me wondering if I will survive this.

"Julio, you should drop the debt so that your beautiful sister here can live," the sharp voice from earlier says as the blade moves down my arm, splitting my skin as it makes its path.

My brother is into something bad. How did he get so deep and not tell us?

There's one thing I learned early in life: never trust a man by word alone. Will these men keep their word? If Julio does what they ask, will they release me?

As the cold blade runs over my exposed breasts, bile rises in my throat, and I fight to swallow it down against my gag. Coughing, I choke. My lips ache from being held open, my arms are numb, and my legs tingle from spending too much time unmoving.

My captor trails the knife down to my stomach. Instinctively, I sit straight up, exposing more of my skin.

"Oh, the stretch marks of pregnancy." He jabs the knife into one of my scars. "How many babies have you had, mamá?" he mocks me as he nicks open each change of my skin. "Uno?"

My stretch marks are a sign of the times my children grew inside me. He's counting them and cutting each one, changing their meaning forever.

Anger builds as my adrenaline pitches higher and higher with each slice of his blade. He is taking my signs of life and killing each one maliciously.

I'm barely holding on. I don't know how much more I can endure.

15

CHAPTER FIFTEEN

LIFE AND DEATH

RUBY

An hour passes, but it feels like a lifetime. Needing to have the connection to Jenna, I am with my kids on the couch in the apartment adjoining mine where Boomer and Pam have been set up. RJ is on the floor, playing with his cars, while Maritza sits beside him with her drawing pad in hand, and Mariella is on my lap.

Maritza speaks first. "Booma says we're gonna camp here tonight."

I look up at my bearded brother and give him a silent nod in thanks. My kids are none the wiser to the situation we are facing. Jenna is a firm believer in kids are meant to be kids. She doesn't want our children to have to grow up too fast like it seems to happen so often in the world today.

From the moment we found out we were pregnant the first time, she laid down the law that adult problems were just that—adult problems. She has done her best over the years, making sure our children don't feel the stress or struggles we have had to endure in order to provide. No matter how angry she got with me, she would refrain until we were alone to avoid making a scene in front of the kids if she could help it. Sometimes, I pushed too hard, and well, shit happened.

Suddenly, the light bulb goes off, and I have this new clarity. For however long now, I have begrudged my wife for changing. But did she really change, or is she being the best damn mom ever? Her fire isn't gone; she simply holds back, because our kids deserve better. Her focus has been them, and I'm the selfish bastard who couldn't see straight. God, I miss my wife.

"Mami needs a night off," Mariella adds. "Ms. Pami called her and left a message not to worry about us. She told Mami to look at the stars tonight so we could talk about what we see in the night sky while we're camping." She lifts up a tiny notepad. "I'm going to draw them for you both. Maritza and I already talked about it. We have a plan." Our daughter beams up at me, and my heart breaks inside.

At least for the night, they can have a normal evening. I don't know what the future holds for us, but they can have this. Camping in the backyard here will be safe. No one who isn't a patched Hellion is making it past the gate of the compound.

"I think she will like knowing what you see tonight."

Maritza comes over and sits beside me. "Papi, there won't be, like, bugs in our tent, right?"

"We'll squash the bugs for you, Ritza," Wesson, one of Pam's boys, pipes in, giving my daughter the reassurance she needs to go outside. She hates bugs and spiders, so this camping thing will be an adventure.

Watching my children get ready for their night out, I can't help hoping and praying that we can somehow find their mother by morning.

After spending some time with them while Boomer sets the tents up, I go back to my place. Waiting is not something I have ever been good at, and tonight is no different. Having had too much time to think and worry, I reach for my phone.

Julio answers on the second ring, his tone sharp. "No time to talk, Ruben."

"Better make time, amigo."

"Or what?" he replies.

"Fucker, I don't know what kind of shit you have brought my family into. At this point, I don't really give a shit other than to know where my wife is so I can bring her home. You need to start talking before my club and I make our way down to you and make you start talking."

"Don't threaten me, Ruben. We've always been on the same side. Don't make that change."

Rage fills me. If he were here right this minute, I would choke the life right out of him.

"Some of your associates drove up on my wife at a gas station. They hit her in the back of the head, knocking her out, Julio. Since we got her out of your father's house, no one, NO ONE, has put their hands on her in harm until your people got to her. Yours! I don't give one fuck about what side you're on. I want to know who these fuckers are so I can rain down the pain and bring my wife home."

He laughs into the phone, and everything inside me runs cold.

"I don't need you and your club to handle my situation. Just sit tight, and I'll have my sister home to you shortly." There is a pause. "That is, if she still wants to come home to you. Ruben, you sure like to throw around the words 'wife' and 'family,' but you know, it wasn't too long ago you didn't want her or that anymore."

"Fuck you!" I cannot believe he's throwing low blows at me right now when Jenna has been taken.

"Like I said, sit tight. I'll handle it."

How in the hell can he think for one second I would sit tight?

"Julio, you're in Mexico. It's only been three hours since they took her. Give up the information so we can get to her"—I pause and quiet my tone—"before it's too late."

"I've got power, Ruben. I've got connections now. I've got this handled." Those are the last words Julio says before the phone goes silent.

Once again, he leaves me helpless.

Ego and pride come before the fall. Only, the person losing the most won't be Julio. It will be me and my children.

She's my life. Slowly, I'm dying inside from not being able to help her. I want to ride out into the night, but I have nowhere to go. Nothing is known.

How do I fight an unknown enemy? How do I track my wife, my life, to an unknown location and face an unknown threat?

The thought of what she's facing kills me. She's my

life, and all of the unknowns are a slow death inside me. Her life hangs in the balance, as does my death. We made a commitment to be one. I may have lost my way for a while, but I see clearly now.

We are one … until death do us part.

Hold strong, Vida. I'm going to find you.

JENNA

Jenna

A fter a few laughs shared amongst the men, the cutting stops. The sounds of retreating footsteps echo around me before silence becomes my comfort.

My body aches, my skin burns, and the bleeding slows and dries in trails down my broken body. I feel gross. My only saving grace right now is that I haven't been raped.

Yet.

Ruby, please come and find me. In my mind, I beg my husband to figure out where I am. I am exhausted. Time has lapsed once again, and I don't know how long I have been gone. Adrenaline and fear are the only things pushing me right now.

Julio is in over his head in something. What, though? We sent money until he sent it back and told me to stop. We talk to him regularly. After his prison time and deportation, I never would have imagined he would get into more trouble. Then again, some people stick to what they know, and what my brother knows is trouble. I can't say he is the type of guy trouble just finds. No, Julio seeks it out like a drug.

He has never used drugs. Sold them, yes. Gotten high, no. He gets off on the rush of getting caught, the power of being in charge. His addiction is the thrill of doing wrong and somehow making it right in his mind.

The man's instruction to drop the debt replays in my mind. My freedom is a trade. If Julio doesn't give in, these men will kill me. Regardless, my death is the only thing I feel is certain.

I bite on the gag and let my tears fall as I think of my children. I think of the many milestones ahead. I think of my girls, my two girls who look just like me and act like Ruben. They are young, too young to be able to remember me. I think of their confirmation dresses for church. I think of their quinceañeras and who will help them find just the right dress. Who will be there to do their hair and place the tiara just right? Who will make the food? We live in America now, so who will plan the parties for them just right? When they get their first real, diamond-studded earrings from Ruben, will he know how to put them in so they don't pinch their ears?

Who will be there to teach my niño, my Ruben

Junior, how to treat a woman when the time comes? Who will be there to hug him and tell him it's okay to cry even if he is a boy? Who will chase away all the whores who try to hold him back in life too early? The way a man grows and treats his mother is a sure sign of his treatment of his wife. What happens if I'm not there to guide my little boy into becoming a man who honors and treasures women?

Then my father comes to my mind. He was taught wrong. He abused his wife and his children. I do not want that for my son. Ruben will set a good example of what a man should become, but RJ still needs the guidance and input of his mother.

I scream against my gag. My heart shatters at the thought of missing even one day with my children. In my mind, the agony of what I could lose is worse than any physical pain these men could put me through.

Will Ruben move on? Will some other woman be Mrs. Castillo? Will she be good to my children? Will she have children of her own? Will he tell my kids about me? Will they keep my memory alive?

No, no, no, Jenna, you cannot go down this road, I tell myself mentally. I did not make it out of my father's hell and the poverty of Mexico just to end up dying naked, tied to a chair. I came to America to have a better life, which means I must live.

I *will* live.

I will be there to watch my son play in his first baseball game. I will be there to watch Mariella win the school spelling bee championship. I will be there to fix Maritza's hair for her middle school dance. Dammit, I will be there for it all.

I'm not signing shit, because I will be the one and only Mrs. Ruben Castillo. There will be no substitute for me with my children. There will be no missed opportunities, no lost memories. No, I don't care what they do to me, and no matter what Julio does or does not do, I will live.

For my babies and for my man, I will get out of this.

I tug and pull against the ties on the chair, only cutting into my skin. The pain merely drives me more. If I can feel, then I am alive, and living is what I have to do until Ruben and the Hellions can find me.

WRONG

RUBY

J ust before dawn, Frisco enters my duplex, and the smirk on his face is one that gives me relief. He has information. Finally, we have something.

I jump up without saying a word.

"What do we know?" I ask immediately.

Tank is grabbing his phone and sending a text when Roundman steps inside behind Frisco.

"They have her in the old shopping center down-town. We hacked into phone records for Julio and traced the number that called in between times of him talking to you, and apparently, he tried to call Jenna before she was attacked."

"When I get my hands on him—"

"Let's get your woman first. Then we'll handle your brother-in-law," Roundman instructs.

I nod my head.

The four of us make our way outside, helmets and bike keys in hand. Making a stop at the cave, we arm ourselves. I'm anxious as we stand around. Then, one by one, my brothers file in, and I realize sermon has been called.

The boys make their way to their spots, and I am shocked to find some of the Catawba Hellions present. It appears as though Tripp, Rex, and Shooter have all made the drive straight here once they got the news. This is family.

While my brother-in-law plays games with the life of his sister, my brothers in the club are ready to ride out and bring her home.

After a quick briefing, we climb on our bikes and pull out. We ride two by two, only feet separating us from one another. One wrong move from any of us would risk us all going down.

Seeing Boomer to my right, I nod my appreciation. I

know his ol' lady Pam will keep the kids safe in their tents. If the situation were reversed, I would want to be beside my brother to bring his woman home.

We make the drive to the old shopping center downtown. What was once a thriving home improvement store is now an empty warehouse. When the mall was built, all the chain stores moved to a better location and all the old buildings have been left behind to rot.

Pulling into the back, we don't hide our presence. Part of me wonders if this is a bad thing. It is my wife who is trapped inside at the mercy of some unknown enemy. Nevertheless, Roundman and Frisco have all the information, and I trust their insight and decisions.

Once Danza yanks the crowbar off the front of his bike and pops the back door open, we each pull out our Glocks then walk in like we own the damn place.

The back space is wide open with concrete floors that are cracked and uneven. My eyes adjust to the darkness just in time to see a single chair off to the side.

In the dim light from the door, I can make out the naked form of my wife, gagged and bleeding, tied to a chair. Blindfolded, her head is up and moving around, and I can see her chest rising and falling heavily as she breathes and probably tries to sort out who is here. The dried blood covering her has me concerned for her injuries and infections.

Immediately, I call out, "Vida," and run to her.

Emotions overwhelm me as I forget everything and everyone around us. Jenna is alive.

She is whimpering and twisting around as I reach her. The other twelve Hellions who made the ride with us move through the building, looking for the guys who have held her, while I focus on my wife.

When I pull off the blindfold, she blinks once, twice, three times, and then her eyes finally find mine and fill with tears. She bites down on her gag as I kneel in front of her and untie it from behind her head. Pulling a knife from my pocket, I cut the zip-ties holding her wrists and ankles in place. She immediately covers herself, so I strip off my cut and shirt to put over her head.

She trembles as I pull her to me, my shirt falling down her body and hitting her knees. She doesn't move her arms into the sleeves; she just falls against me, shaking.

I kiss the top of her head. "Vida, I'm here."

Boomer stands behind me and clears his throat. "We need to get Doc Kelly to look her over."

Head Case and his ol' lady Doc Kelly are both doctors. They followed us in Boomer and Pam's van since we didn't know what state we would find Vida in. He is a shrink, and she is a physician, both for the club and in general practice for the Catawba Hellions.

I pull away from my wife who looks up at me, and I break into a million pieces.

"Can Doc Kelly check you out?"

Jenna nods her head and steps away from me. She is in shock; that is evident.

As the small, brunette doctor comes around me with her backpack of medical supplies, I move to the side so she can wrap her arm around Jenna's shoulders and guide her away from the crowd.

My instincts scream at me to stand beside my wife, but the look in her eyes tells me this has been a hell she doesn't want to relive in front of me.

There is a commotion sounding from the store front, pulling my attention away from Jenna. Not long after, Roundman, Danza, Frisco, Tripp, and Rex come in with three Hispanic men in front of them, zip-tied with their hands behind their backs. The men are muttering to each other in Spanish not to speak about the boss or the debt.

Walking to them, I wrap my hands around the throat of the first one I reach. "Respuesta! ¡Hablaras!" I order him to speak.

"Julio Natera?"

"Respuesta!" I again tell him he's wrong as I tighten my grip, cutting off his air supply.

"Get Vida situated to go home. We'll handle these three until you get her on her way," Roundman says as he shoves one of the guys forward.

He's right; she's been through enough. I need to get her home before showing these chuckleheads just how wrong they were to ever target my family to resolve their debts.

The sounds of the bikes pulling up have me ready to sigh in relief, knowing Ruben and the Hellions are here.

In the same moment, panic fills me. What if it's not them? I'm stuck, completely helpless, but I have to believe it is Ruby.

I twist my head and fight my rapid breathing as I hear the door being busted open and the footsteps entering my space. Lots of footsteps.

Fear grips me. Naked and unable to see what's coming, I feel like I may hyperventilate.

"Vida," Ruby says, and my heart skips a beat. The feeling of safety fills me from his voice.

Ruben is here and no matter what, he will get me home to my babies. Emotions overwhelm me, and my body trembles involuntarily.

He removes my blindfold. With the dim lighting in the room, it is hard for me to adjust, and I have to blink multiple times. Within a few moments, he has me covered in his shirt and over in a corner with Doc Kelly.

"Jenna, I need to check your eyes first since you sustained a head injury. The cuts need to be cleaned, but we will get you home first."

I hold my head up and open my eyes to stare blankly at the wall behind her. Then she moves the light from one eye to the next. Satisfied with whatever my reaction is, she leans in closely.

Whispering, she asks, "Do we need to perform a rape kit?"

I choke back tears and shake my head.

"Jenna, whatever you say stays between us. I won't tell Ruben if you don't want me to. I need to know, though, so you are examined thoroughly."

Opening my mouth, it takes a minute to get words. Everything burns, and my mouth is so dry.

"They hurt me," I croak, "but not like that."

"Are you sure? Even when you were knocked out?"

The room spins, and I feel like I'm going to pass out. I have been so caught up in everything happening to me in the moment that I haven't given myself time to really assess what happened while I was unconscious.

"Breathe, Jenna. You've gotta breathe."

I exhale loudly and try to steady myself.

"Let's get you to the car. You're dehydrated, so we need to get an IV in you and go from there first."

I nod my head while I watch in the distance as Ruben wraps his hand around some stranger's neck. I can feel the rage coming off my husband from this distance.

Fear has a way of changing one's perspective on violence. After I sat here, afraid for my future, there is no amount of pain that could be inflicted that would make me have any sympathy for those men.

It's all so wrong. Why take me? I have nothing to do with my brother's business in Mexico. There are still so many questions, but in this moment, I don't care about the answers. I want to get home and get cleaned up so I can hug each of my children. I just might never let them go.

Everything is a blur as Ruben comes over and then rides with me in the van as Head Case follows behind us on Ruben's bike. My throat tightens, anxiety gripping me as we pull into the driveway.

"My babies," I panic. "They can't see me like this." I don't want them to see a light on at the house from where they are at Boomer and Pam's and think they can come home. I would never turn them away, but I do not want them to be scared or upset.

"Compound camping." Ruben says as he gets out and extends his hand for me to follow. "Boomer and

Pam made this big deal of you having a night off. We can go and get them later. Boomer is on his way back, so when they wake up, they won't know anyone was even gone."

I let out a relieved sigh as we make our way inside. My body feels like I have fire running through my veins.

"We need to clean you up and see if you need stitches. We also need to get you hydrated," Doc Kelly says as she moves into my kitchen and opens her bag.

Ruben takes me by the hand, guiding me through the house. "We can do this in the bathroom."

He sits me on the toilet and I wince. The more I get comfortable in my surroundings, the more the adrenaline wears off, and I feel the crash coming.

I watch as Ruben gets a bowl and washcloth to begin cleaning me. He's reaching up to my face when I start to panic.

"No!" I scream and jerk back from his touch. "This is wrong. Everything is wrong!" I inhale sharply. "You can't come and save me then think it's your place to take care of me. Go away, Ruben. Go the fuck away!" My throat burns. My eyes feel like someone is pricking them with a straight pin because I have no tears left to cry when my body wants to.

"Vida," Ruben whispers, and I can see the hurt in his eyes at my rejection.

"No! Vida nothing. I was scared, Ruben. You were scared. Nothing changes, though. You don't love me." I sob. "You. Don't. Love me."

He drops to his knees in front of me. "I'm so sorry, Vida. I messed up what we had because I was looking for something I thought was lost. It was me. It was my issue. I failed us, and I did wrong. I allowed myself to question something good until I convinced myself it was something bad. I was wrong." He looks up at me, his eyes pleading for forgiveness. "I failed you twice. I promise you, with everything I am, I will spend my every breath for the rest of my days by your side. Ride or die, you're it for me. I've had time to realize, when I say you are my Vida, you *are* my life. You are me. We are one."

Without the energy to fight, I drop my head on top of his. "This is wrong."

"No, Vida. Me and you together, that's always right. I was wrong to ever think there is anything better than me and you, baby."

I want to believe him. I want to know, just as I have seen where I failed us, he can see his shortcomings, too. I want to believe that, out of so many wrongs, we can find something right again.

17

CHAPTER SEVENTEEN

WALLS

R_UBY_

"Ruby," Doc Kelly calls from the doorway of our bathroom, holding a bottle of whiskey. "Why don't you give me some time with Jenna?"

Feeling defeated, I stand, and as I cross paths with the doctor, I reach out for the bottle.

She smiles at me. "Not for you."

"I don't drink," Jenna immediately replies, looking at Doc Kelly.

"Once we get the IV in you, I need to scrape the cut in your shoulder and then stitch it up. Since it has partially tried to heal, this means reopening the wound. You're gonna want a little something to take the edge off, babe."

Rage fills me.

"I'll be back. Gonna take a ride." Going over to my wife, I kiss her forehead, seeing the distance she's trying to keep between us in her eyes.

Healing both physically and emotionally will take some time, and not just from her ordeal the last twelve hours, but from the damage done by me. She needs to know where I'm at with her and with us.

"I love you, Vida. Build whatever walls you need to, but brick by brick, I'll tear them down. I'm not, nor have I ever been, afraid of hard work. I'll see you later. Rest when you can."

She takes in my words and nods her head. I reach the bathroom doorway before she croaks out a reply.

"Make them pay, Ruben."

I turn around and again am hit by the pain in her eyes. It cuts me to my very core.

"For you, for me, and for our children, mi amor," I answer her as I exit.

The ride back to the old storefront only amps me up

further. I will fight to the bitter end to get back what I walked away from. I want my life with Jenna back. Only, now I know it will be better than ever because I am aware.

I am aware I have shortcomings as a man.

I am aware I am human and will fail.

What defines me is how I overcome my failures. I will be defined as the man who stands for and by my family.

Pausing, I blow out a breath before climbing off my bike and making my way inside to my club and my enemies.

At the door, standing watch is Tank, stopping me before I enter.

"Your brother-in-law—"

"This isn't about him in this moment."

"I get that, brother, but you've gotta know. He's in deep across the border."

This is not what I wanted to hear, but I will deal with Julio later. Right now, there are three men on the other side of this door who kidnapped, assaulted, and sliced my wife. They attacked my family, and they will pay tonight.

Walking in, I find the guys are tied to chairs in the same fashion as Vida, although with their clothes on. This isn't about manipulation or humiliation; this is about retribution. I'm not here to solve the issue with

Julio. That is his business. I'm here purely to inflict pain.

"We didn't know," one of the men stutters.

"Yeah," the third adds while the man in the middle remains silent, hanging his head down. "We didn't know she was an ol' lady to the Hellions."

The first guy looks at me. "We didn't know she was your wife."

Standing in front of him, I wrap my hands around his throat. "She's more than my wife." I choke him harder. He fights to breathe as I tighten around his windpipe, pressing my thumbs in. His face changes colors as his eyes grow big. "She's my life," I say, meeting him eye to eye as I apply more pressure.

His two friends watch as I continue to squeeze long after their man has passed out.

"She's my partner, my other half. She's my reason, and you touched her," I say over him as his body goes limp.

I press my thumbs in deeper and grip more tightly. I squeeze the life out of him as I let my mind focus on the worries and pain my wife endured at the hands of these men. No resuscitation will be had tonight.

Next.

Roundman stands in front of the second guy, the man who will not meet my eyes. I can tell by my brothers' reactions this is the one with the debt to Julio.

I move past him and go to the third man in the lineup. Taking the knife Rex has extended to me, I look over the metal in my hand.

"You and your amigos"—I look to the man in the middle chair—"felt it necessary to take a blade to my wife's body." I trace the blade down the third man's face, splitting his skin enough to burn and bleed yet not going deeply … yet. He whimpers, but he doesn't cry out. "You and your amigos felt it necessary to cut into my wife's skin. You and your amigos felt it necessary to take my wife away from our children and our family to avoid a debt. In doing this, you and your amigos felt it necessary to bring pain to the mother of my children." I can't help raising my voice as I continue to speak, the rage burning deep inside me. "If only I could find your mothers and reign down my retribution on their bodies..."

I pause, backing up. "But in our culture, we don't do that. My mother was cherished, protected until her very last breath. You and your amigos didn't respect where we come from. You pathetic pieces of shit used a woman as a pawn for your debts." Swinging, I step forward and plunge the knife into the stomach of the third man.

He grunts and looks up at me as I twist the metal in his body.

"Was it fun to make my wife bleed?" I ask as I yank

the knife out and plunge it back in again. "Do you feel the fear of what will happen to you next? Do you sit here and ask yourself, 'how long until I am free of the pain?' "

The man in the middle continues to look down while his buddy slumps in the chair, mumbling incoherently in pain as his blood pools onto the floor beneath him.

"That's what my wife did for the hours you had her. From the moment she woke up after you took her from the gas station, she had to ask herself what was next." I rip the knife free and stab the man again, this time in the ribs. "She had to helplessly wonder if she would ever see our babies again."

I pull the knife free and jab it into his other side. "I had to sit and wait while my brothers here had to use resources to find out who took her. I had to wonder if I would see my wife, my Vida, again." I yank the knife out while the man in front of me chokes on his own blood and his head lolls from side to side.

Leaving him to bleed out, I move to where Roundman is standing and watching the man in the middle. I force the man to lift his head by taking the tip of the bloody knife and putting it under his chin. When his eyes meet mine, I ask, "Do you have any idea what that does to a man?"

I watch as the man swallows hard, but he doesn't speak. I give a sinister smile.

"It makes him go loco." I laugh. "The thing is, as crazy as I may be, I'm not stupid. You see, dumb fucker, your debt is to Julio Natera. If I kill you, the debt will not be repaid in money, markers, or in whatever way Julio desires. I've had my vengeance.

"What do you think being in another country and knowing his sister was taken did to Julio? It drove me loco in a matter of minutes. I can only imagine what it did to him. Now you get sent back to Mexico. You are Julio's problem."

Rex and Tripp laugh, and I look beneath the man's seat to see he has pissed himself. As much as I want to kill the man, I don't want to take care of his problem in any way. Julio can deal with how to make him pay.

Knowing Roundman and the Hellions will handle getting this clown back to Mexico, I hand the knife back to Rex. I have walls to climb at home to get back to my wife's heart.

As I reach the exit door, I look at Boomer. "I'll be by to get my kids later. As for this, when they get him out, you do what you do. Make it go boom, brother."

Jenna

D oc Kelly wasn't kidding. The shots of whiskey did take the edge off when it came to getting my shoulder scraped clean then stitched. Since we didn't know what happened to me while I was knocked out, she did a rape kit, but there were no signs indicating I was violated in that manner.

Thank God for small blessings. This whole ordeal was bad enough on its own.

Julio, my brother, got me into this mess, and I don't even know why. Does it matter, though?

My phone and my van aren't here, so after Doc Kelly cleaned me up, she recommended I rest until later when Ruben brings my kids home.

I want nothing more than to see them, hold them, kiss them, and know they are really with me. Still, I have spent their entire lives sheltering them from so many dangers of the world, but this is something I can't hide, and I don't know what to tell them.

After Doc Kelly gets my IV set up, I allow myself to drift to sleep. My body aches, the exhaustion from everything taking over. Being in my own home and knowing Doc Kelly and Head Case are part of the Hellions' family, I am safe.

"Vida." I hear Ruby's whispered voice. I am not fully awake yet not completely asleep. "I know I put you through hell, baby. I got lost in my head. I played the shoulda, coulda, woulda game that always ends in disappointment. You know, before this happened, I was ready and wanting to work things out. I need another chance. I need our life back, my wife back."

Two strong arms pull me over. Except, instead of lying on his back and draping me over him, Ruben Castillo cocoons himself around me.

In his warmth, in his love, I fall into a deep sleep, the kind fairytales are made of.

Can I trust that he will be a prince of his own making? Can I believe we will have our happily ever after?

There is one thing I learned from being taken: I have to hold on to myself. When no one else was there, I had to pull through, not just for my man and my kids, even though they drive me, but for me. I can't get sucked back into the wash of the day in and out routine. I can't simply be my children's mother and my husband's wife. I have to be me and live for me. I have to find a way to take care of myself so I can take care of the needs of those around me.

Ruben's way of handling all the changes between us may not have been the easiest of roads—it hurt like hell —but the end of the path is still the same, isn't it?

Ride or die, we do it together.

In this journey, I learned it hurts my man and my family as a whole when I simply lie down and push through everything to merely get to the next task. I learned I am more than the caretaker of our household.

I am vital.

I am who I am, and I am loved for me exactly as I am, flawed and all. It's okay to ask for more from my husband and my friends. It's okay, when the time is right, to pick my battles and fight for what I want and need. It's not okay to simply accept this is how it has to be. It's not okay to think those around me will simply play along, waiting for some change to happen. This is not fake it until you make it. This is life, and it's time to live it.

I'm not sure how much time passes before I finally wake up. Stretching, I realize Ruben isn't with me. More than that, I ache. Doc Kelly wasn't kidding about feeling worse than after having a baby. My body was made to accomplish that; it was not made to be tied up and used for a cutting board.

It takes a little more time than usual to dress, but once I get up and moving, I want nothing more than to see my babies.

"Vida," Ruben says from the kitchen, carrying a glass of milk. He watches me like he thinks I'm going to break.

"I need to see my kids, Ruben."

He nods. "They're at Boomer and Pam's now."

I swallow the apprehension that's building. "What are we going to tell them? I don't want them to be scared their tio's business will bring them harm."

"Roundman is going today to pick you up a brand new SUV. We've been wanting a bigger vehicle, anyway. He knows a guy who can get us a deal on a Suburban. We can explain the bruising, cuts, and pain by saying you were in a mild car accident."

I nod my head. "I'm good with that." I don't want my children to worry, and I am happy to not see my van again. I don't think I would be comfortable in it anymore.

He smiles when he reaches me. When he hands me the glass of milk and a Tylenol, I laugh.

"I know you won't want anything stronger than this, but you need to take something to at least take the edge off."

I smile back. "Gonna take care of me, are you?"

"For the rest of my life," Ruben answers immediately before leaning down and brushing his lips to mine. "Let's go and get our kids."

"Thank you," I whisper.

"For what?"

"Saving me, pushing me, and more than anything, staying by my side. I know things have been a mess for a long time, not just since the separation. When they had me, though, I knew you would fight to find me. I never doubted you."

He wraps his arms around me. "Don't say stuff that makes me want to take you to bed and spend hours lost inside you when we need to get you to our babies so you can hug them and give them all that mami squishy shit you do." He kisses my forehead. "Thank you for always staying by my side and never doubting I would come through for you."

Hand in hand, Ruben and I make our way over to Boomer and Pam's. We don't knock; we walk right in, and the sight has me folding over, laughing.

In the recliner is Nathan 'Boomer' Vaughn with his head back and a pirate hat on his head, a Nerf gun on his lap, and my two girls at his feet, painting his toenails while he sleeps. Pam is in the kitchen, sipping coffee and watching the mayhem. The boys are all playing cars down the hallway that has become their own drag strip.

RJ makes it to me first. "Mami, I tried to keep him manly with the gun and the hat," he explains.

The girls carefully put the lids on their pink and neon-green nail polishes before making their way to me.

Maritza reaches me with a smile. "We went camping. Booma said whoever fell asleep first would get shaving cream on their face or markers. Well, we all fell asleep at the same time. Then Booma brought us home, but Mami, he couldn't stay awake, so Mariella and I decided we would have some sleepover fun."

Boomer rubs his eyes as he wakes up and looks down at his toes. My girls glance up, wondering if he's going to be mad, but the bearded beast of a man starts laughing at himself.

"Guess I earned this one."

"Your secret is safe with us, Booma," Ruben mocks with a smile.

I breathe in and out. When was the last time we could be with friends together and laugh? It's been far too long. We have tall walls to climb over, but with love, we can conquer anything.

ONE DAY AT A TIME

RUBY

C hildren are resilient, they say. I am a believer now. Surprisingly, they haven't questioned the accident. They have merely spent the last few days helping to care for their injured mother.

As each day passes, Vida starts to feel better, and we find a routine together. Still, apprehension fills me. I am home with my wife and my children, but will she make me leave again?

She has needed me to help her shower, bandage her wounds, and take care of the kids. As she gets stronger, I find myself wondering when this will all come to an end.

She steps out of the shower on her own and is moving to the closet to get dressed when I walk into our room, not thinking. The towel covering her body moves, and I can see the still healing marks on her abdomen.

They caused her pain. *I* caused her pain. It kills me knowing all that she has had to endure because of me, because of her brother, and because we have failed her.

"Vida," I whisper as my heart breaks into a million pieces.

She looks at me, not understanding. "Are you okay, Ruby?"

I reach out and pull her to me. Surprisingly, she falls into my embrace freely.

"Life," I whisper, kissing the top of her head. "You gave me life."

Her arms wrap around my waist, and I feel whole once again.

"Ruby," she whispers.

"Shh, just let me hold you."

I need her in my arms. I need to know I have her back. I need to feel her safe … with me. I haven't always done right by her, and the future is unknown, but one thing is for sure: I will make mistakes. I am a man. I am a flawed man. But with everything I am, I love this woman.

"Vida, mi amor."

She grips me more tightly.

"I'm sorry, Jenna. I'm sorry for hurting you, hurting us. I'm sorry I wasn't there for you. I'm sorry they ever got to you. I'm sorry you hurt." As emotions overwhelm me, I drop to my knees in front of her.

The towel falls as she rests her hands on my shoulders and watches me. Her skin is red with parts scabbed over in healing. Gently, I run my fingers over her marred stretch marks.

"I know you are raw inside and out. I know the wounds cut deeper than the skin. I know this will take time." I look to her eyes. "I beg you, Vida, don't push me out. Give me a second chance. Give *us* a second chance."

Tears fill her eyes as I trace each mark done to her. Sadness and anger fill me as I look at the inflamed skin. The very skin that has been stretched and bore the mark of giving life and is now marred by the damage of another man's greed.

"Lo siento, mi amor, lo siento," I apologize to her as I continue to run my fingers over the marks. "You gave me life in more ways than one. When they had you, I had to face the thought of a life without you, and Jenna, there is none. Without you, there is no me, and I can see clearly now you are my future; you are my past; you are my life. I don't want to be without you."

She cups my face in her hand, her thumb running over the gem tattoo under my eye. "Ruben Castillo, you are a beautiful man." She smiles softly. "You light a fire inside me hotter than anyone else. You drive me crazy, drive me wild, and you keep me grounded. You have the power to hurt me more than anyone in the world."

I try to drop my head in shame, but she holds me firmly.

"You are my Ruby, my gem. You are my heat, my passion, and you are my life.

"While they had me, I tried to think of your life without me. I tried to think of our kids, and it killed me, Ruben, but it also gave me the power to hold strong. You give me that. You give me the power to be me, even when I want to stab you sometimes."

When I lean in and kiss her belly, she tenses, which reminds me of her injuries. We can't be rushed. Healing can't be rushed.

"I don't know what the future holds, but I do know I don't want it to be without you and our kids. I want our family to be together," I say, uncertain where she is going with everything.

"No one knows what the future holds, Ruby. We

have to ride the rocky path together. We have to enjoy the smooth times and hold tight to each other on the curves and every bump along the way. It's not going to be easy, so we have to take it one day at a time."

Relief fills me, heat warms me, and love consumes me.

Picking up the towel, I wrap it around her as I stand.

"I love you, Jenna Mariella Castillo." I brush my lips to hers. "My Vida." I kiss her again.

Slowly, she opens her mouth, and I take her bottom lip between mine. Then I trace a line with my tongue as her hands come up to my neck. She rubs the place where Vida is tattooed while I deepen our kiss. Softly, our tongues meet, and sparks fly through me.

I feel the heat.

I feel the love.

I feel it all.

She does this to me. She has this power over me. No one else, only her: my wife, my life, my Vida.

Jenna

Life is a rollercoaster of ups and downs. I think back to riding the Dragon's Tail with Ruben and the many curves along the way. Our life is a lot like that ride: a lot of holding on; depending on each other; and finding the joy, even in the scariest of times.

It's a Hellions rite of passage to take the eleven mile course with over three hundred curves. It's an honor as an ol' lady to ride it with your man. You have to trust him and his brothers as you go through the mountain, two by two, on the winding and narrow road.

Just like that ride, I know I can trust our Hellions MC family in life. I can trust that Ruben and I have both found our way. It won't be easy, and there will be a lot of rebuilding to do between us, but we are better together than we are apart.

In some ways it seems crazy to take him back. I

have to ask myself if I can handle that level of pain again should it all far apart. At the end of the day, though, I also have to ask myself do I want to lose the man I have given it all to on a chance that he could break my heart and miss out on what could be an amazing future. What doesn't kill us only makes us stronger. Going through the loss, getting taken, and not knowing whether I would see him or my children again has strengthened me. I know myself. I am aware of how easy it is to lose myself into my roles as wife and mother. I won't do that again. When I ask myself what I can and can't survive, I know I can make it through should it all fall apart again. What I can't overcome is the questions I would always wonder if I walked away and didn't give us a second chance.

Ruben leaves me to get dressed after sharing a soft, slow kiss together, and then I stand in the closet and stare at its mostly empty contents.

I smile to myself. Just like this closet, without Ruben, I am missing something. I am me always. I can stand on my own, and nothing will fall, but I am not full unless I have him. This very closet that contains our clothes is not full without the two of us becoming one together, mixing ourselves and blending our lives into one complete unit.

There have been many times I have packed Ruben's things, just to set them outside when, deep in my heart, I knew I would take him back. Now, as I stand in this closet and look at his missing items, I realize that, each time I was packing him up, I was doing it knowing he still belonged beside me.

I pull down my clothing and dress with the hopes that my husband will soon return his things to where they belong, and never again will our closet or our lives have to be half full.

When I make my way to the kitchen, I can't help laughing. Ruben has all three kids at the table with their bowls in front of him. On the countertop, I see seven boxes of cereal lined up, and five of them have already been opened. Ruben is pouring another bowl when he stops and sees me.

"Take your pick." He smirks and gestures to the boxes.

"That's not how this works," I joke.

"See? I told you Mami would only let us open one box at a time. The cereal can go bad if we don't eat it right away," Maritza pipes up first while RJ drops his head.

"Umm…" Ruben says, and then he reaches out and pulls me to him. "I can't cook, Vida. They didn't need to eat the same thing three meals a day," he whispers.

I can't stop myself from laughing. "Who has been making me soup and sandwiches, then, if you guys have had to eat cereal?"

"Pami," Mariella is the first to answer. "Booma and Pami have been bringing over food for you and all of us. Papi just keeps offering cereal. So, vegetables or cereal, what would you pick?"

I laugh as I lean into Ruben. "It's a good thing Mami is feeling better, then, so we can get back to eating right and not just sugar and milk."

"Aw, man," RJ whines. "I like when Papi is in charge."

Ruben laughs, and then everything gets quiet.

"Is Papi going to have to leave again since you're feeling better, Mami?" Maritza asks, and my heart breaks that my children have felt this pain.

"Sometimes, you have to take some time to breathe to learn just how good you have it," Ruben begins to explain.

I decide they are young, so I interject with the easiest of replies. "Papi is home, and everything is good between us. Don't worry yourselves over it. Just know your papi is home."

As he smiles down at me, my life feels like it is beginning again. Our kids are healthy, happy, and satisfied with my answer. My man is home, healthy, happy, and he's in love with me. I am alive, home, and I found myself again.

Life is good. We just have to take it all one day at a time.

CHAPTER NINETEEN

19

MRS. CASTILLO

RUBY

ONE MONTH LATER

My phone rings, making my adrenaline automatically kick in when I see the name on the display.

"Julio," I answer sharply.

"Mi hermana is not answering my calls; why? I got your gift," he says, referring to the debtor returned to him. "I have reached out since finding out Jenna is safe. Why is she not answering me?"

Damn right she's not. When his life invaded ours, my wife decided that is a danger she will not have our children subjected to. She made the decision to cut her brother off, and I support it.

"We're done, Julio. She's not answering because she's done. I'm done. We're done."

"The hell we are! We're family. You owe me."

I owe him? What the hell is he thinking? Has he been smoking the dope he's been selling? It's a good thing he's in Mexico, because if he were here, I would drain the life from his body myself.

"I don't owe you shit."

"You failed my sister."

"I failed!" I yell, not holding back. "I vowed to be her protector and her provider. It wasn't my danger that came to her doorstep. The blowback was on you! I take care of what's mine."

He laughs into the phone, only angering me further. "Is she yours?"

"Jenna Mariella Castillo is and always has been my Vida. She is the first and only Mrs. Ruben Castillo," I clip out at him. "You know how our culture is, and you should have protected her. You. Failed. A Natera, she is no more."

"Don't you—"

"Don't I, what?" I goad. "It's my calls she answers. It's my arms she finds safety in. It's my life she shares in. We are the Castillos, and the next time your shit finds its way into my world, it's the last time, for the ties will be severed in death—yours."

He mutters something in shock before he says, "Don't you threaten me."

"It's a promise, not a threat."

"I've never had a problem with the Hellions. Don't make there be one now, Ruby."

It's my turn to laugh. "The moment your business crossed into our territory, you had a problem. My loyalty to you was over after your man was delivered. That is the last marker I'll ever give you."

"Stop this, amigo."

"Listen, Julio, and listen carefully," I instruct, pausing to make sure I have his attention. "We're done. Jenna is done with you. She's Mrs. Castillo, ol' lady in the Hellions MC. Make sure your people know she's untouchable. The next time—should there ever be one —you'll pay the price."

He says nothing, and knowing my message has been received, I end the call.

Julio is in deep back home, running his own territory. He has found some way to smuggle drugs here to the US, which has been profitable for him. However, standing on his own two feet in a life of crime has come at a price: his family. I cannot stand here and say my hands are clean. I cannot say the club I claim is on the up and up as far as the laws of our nation go. What I can say is, for every crime that has been committed, it has been followed through based on a code. I cannot say the same for Julio.

He once was at a crossroad, and he followed the wrong path. Julio is driven by power and greed. The Hellions and the life I lead are driven by family. I am never alone, and I am never in need. I don't have to watch my back; my brothers will do it for me.

Julio will never have this. He will never sleep easy at night, knowing his woman is safe. He's too far gone. There's no turning back for him or for me.

Once upon a time, long ago when we were two young men, Julio and I were at a crossroads together. We watched as Juan lost his life to the violence of gang life in Mexico.

How can they call that family when, day in and day out, people are dying, some by the hands of their so-called amigos?

We fought hard to get away from the temptation of drugs and easy money. We worked hard to pave a new path here in America.

When we came to the next crossroad in life together, Julio chose a different direction from me. We both picked a road less traveled with many curves and bumps along the way. He wasn't so far misguided that he couldn't have found a better way; he just didn't.

The next crossroad Julio came to, he took the road that seemed to be paved in gold, the road that seemed to offer so much. Only, in the end, he took the road that led to nowhere.

When he can allow his troubles to find their way to his sister and possibly her children, he has lost control. No matter how he sees it, he has. My kids could have been with Jenna that night. That thought alone has me rattled all over again.

He has made his choices, and he has to live with those consequences. I have made mine, and although I have made mistakes along the way, I will forever protect and provide for Jenna. She is my life, for now and for always.

My mind goes back to when Julio and Jenna were once my only family.

The mass seems to go on forever. It's my mother's service, her funeral service.

I need a drink—tequila. I will even down the worm to drown the pain inside me.

The Hail Mary's go on for far too long before I can finally get outside where I immediately unbutton the top button of my dress shirt and look to the Heavens.

"Lo siento, Mama," I mutter for not wearing a tie and suit coat. I feel like I'm suffocating enough

without her, much less if I had choked myself with a tie.

A firm grip on my shoulder tells me Julio followed me out of the church. I hug my best friend and take comfort in not being alone.

"She was a good woman, a strong woman," he says to me, and I nod my head, knowing every word is true.

"The only family I had."

Jenna, who followed her brother, looks up at me. "You have us, Ruben." She reaches up to cup my face in her soft, small hands, her thumb resting under my eye. "You have me and Julio." She smiles with tears in her eyes. "Ruby"—her thumb moves in small circles under my eye—"you are your mom's gem. You are not alone. She's always with you." She pulls my face down to hers and kisses the spot under my eye where she had her thumb.

The next day, I went and had the ruby gem tattooed under my eye in the very spot she kissed me, the very spot she named me my mother's gem. She made a vow to my mother that day that I wouldn't be alone, and she kept her word.

I look to the Heavens now. "Lo siento, Mamá," I apologize again.

If she were still alive, she would be ashamed of me. She would be angered at the hurt I caused my wife. She would be saddened that I turned my back on my vows.

Tears prick at my eyes, but I refuse to let them fall.

She once told me when I was a boy that I would one day find a woman and make her my wife. When the time came that I made that commitment, I would then make my own family and would need to make them my focus.

When you have so little in life, it's hard to let go.

Julio has made his choices, and I have to put my family first. I made a commitment to Jenna. I made babies with her. I have to keep them safe.

Julio and Jenna stood by me when I had nothing. Together, we worked hard to be where we are today. Only, where he is doesn't protect where we are, so the time has come to let him go.

I sigh. "I'm trying. I'm trying," I mutter to the sky. "Mamá, you raised me to be a man of honor and integrity. I'm going to give every part of me to my wife and our family, no holding back." I make the promise to my mother's angel and to myself.

I will be my mother's gem, and I will be the man my wife has always treasured.

Jenna

I t's funny how sometimes, when you tear something completely apart and then put it back together, it seems to be stronger than ever before. I have to pinch myself to believe how far my husband and I have come.

I can't say it's been easy, because it hasn't. I have tried to push him away, but at night when the bad dreams come, he's there to chase them away. He holds me and reminds me I'm safe in his arms.

Pam comes in my house, taking me from my thoughts of my night-terror problems. The boys run in and straight to RJ's room. Mariella and Maritza are most likely going to join them. Then it won't be long before my house will be overrun with toys and the noise of children playing.

It's my every dream come true. My babies are safe at home, playing without a care in the world.

She starts to unload the grocery bags of baking supplies she has brought over. Today, we are baking cookies, lots and lots of cookies. Between the two of us, we have five kids and five adults living in our homes. Then we both work for the club where Pam cleans the offices and houses while I do mini-storage work. Therefore, we are going to make some for the businesses and our families.

Before we start, Pam looks at me, studying me.

"What?" I ask, wondering what she's thinking.

"How are you really? Don't give me the, 'Ruby, I'm fine' bullshit answer, either. He may buy it, but I know better than that."

I smile at my friend. "I'm all over the place."

"Wanna talk about it?"

I lay out ingredients and start measuring. "I don't know where to begin."

She gets the eggs out of my fridge. "How are you today?"

"Confused and scared."

"You know that's normal, right?"

"I don't know anything anymore." I sigh then let out my biggest fear. "My brother is so in over his head with what he considers his drug empire in Mexico that it came back on me. What if they go after my kids? This happened because of my brother!"

"My children's sperm donor was a malicious man, and unlike you, I subjected my kids to living in that."

I reach out and squeeze Pam's arm, knowing the hell she once lived with her ex-husband and why she ran away. "It's not your fault. Don't let the guilt get to you."

Pam sacrificed herself by being separated from her children for their safety. Now, though, my friend has found her happily ever after and safety for herself and her children with Boomer and the Hellions MC.

She meets my gaze, and I can see the tears in her eyes. "My kids have seen too much for their young ages. The hardest part, is trusting yourself again."

"I've been avoiding Julio because I don't want to be the dumb girl who believes everything her brother tells her. He's going to lie to me. I'll never know the whole truth about what he's involved in and why it found its way to me."

She leans against my counter. "Do you want to deal with him?"

I look to her and pause before looking to my phone. Without giving myself time to second-guess, I dial my brother.

The cockiness in his voice sends chills down my spine.

"Well, well, well, she does remember how to use the phone. You should know your spouse threatened my life, so I'm not sure this phone call is permitted."

I am in shock. Ruben talked to Julio and threatened him? My mind races. Of course he did. Julio is the reason I was taken.

"How bad, Julio?" I get right to the point.

"How bad, what? How bad will I make your spouse pay for his betrayal? Well, that depends, baby sister."

My stomach burns and anger consumes me. "Don't you turn this around! I was calling in hopes my brother, the one who protected me from our father, the one who took care of me while he was gone, and the one who brought me to a land of freedom, would be able to reassure me that, whatever he's into, it won't harm my children the way it did me."

"You should know that hopes lead to disappointments," he answers cryptically.

It's one thing to have to face down every fear. It's one thing to have to be stripped, tied, and gagged. It's one thing to be a carving station for some asshole. It is another thing entirely to even fathom I have to worry about my children being in danger.

"You should know then that I'm Jenna Mariella Castillo, ol' lady in the Hellions Motorcycle Club. You should know it's not a hope; it's a given that my children are protected. They are safe in the arms of the family Ruben and I made for ourselves."

"Oh, so the little American princess is too good for her spic brother now?"

Tears fill my eyes, but I won't back down.

"That's not it at all, Julio, and you know it. If that's what you have to tell yourself to ease your conscious that you couldn't protect what you once considered family, that's your shortcoming."

He pauses before replying, "It was a debt owed to me. I never thought you would be a target."

"If you ever cared about me and my family at all, then you'll understand I have to walk away, Julio. I have to make sure we are never a target again."

He says nothing for a beat, and then his answer is simple. "Understood, Mrs. Castillo." Those are the last words my brother speaks before disconnecting the call without giving me an opportunity to say anything else.

I look at Pam. "I'm good now."

"What did you take away from that call?"

I smile, my heart filling with pride. "I am Jenna Castillo, Ruby's ol' lady in the Hellions MC. I have family, I have my man, and I am safe."

CHAPTER TWENTY

PLANTING SEEDS

Ruby

ONE YEAR LATER

The fire is burning hot in our life now. Walking into the house after work and seeing Jenna behind the stove with her long, black hair braided down her back, my dick gets hard. It's another day in paradise.

Life is calm. Life is good. Life is with my wife.

Moving behind her, I wrap my hands around her

waist and drop my head to her neck where I suck ... hard.

She laughs, and I swear I'm in heaven.

"I'm one lucky motherfucker. I've got a wife who's hot as hell, can cook, and gives me beautiful babies," I whisper before nibbling her earlobe.

"Ruby," she whispers, "the babies."

"The babies will see me loving their mama. They will see how real love is treasured. They will see me hold you and kiss you and tell you just how much you mean to me."

She giggles, and my dick presses against the zipper of my jeans.

"Give me ten minutes to see if I can grow our family by one more," I tease.

She huffs playfully. "You want me barefoot and pregnant?"

"I want my seed so deep inside of you we make life together." I rock into her and trail my hands up her sides to cup her breasts through her shirt. "I want to see your body grow with our life once again. I love you pregnant. I love you not pregnant. I love you as the mother of my children. I love you as my wife. More than anything, Jenna Mariella Castillo, I love you. I love you so much I want to create life with you, because mi amor, you are my Vida."

She leans back into me and wiggles her ass against

my erection. "I have to feed the life we already created, but if you are a lucky man, you will get the chance to make a new life tonight." She flicks her spatula up at me. "Now out of my kitchen; I have a family to cook for." She smiles at me when I push away.

Reluctantly, I go to our room. Deciding I need to clean up before I ravage my wife, I take a cold shower and change into some sweats. When I come back out, the kids are already at the table, so I take my place and smile as I watch my wife fill her plate to sit down and eat … all of us together.

There was a time when this didn't seem like enough. I was a selfish, greedy man to not find satisfaction, complete satisfaction, in this: three beautiful children; a wife who, through thick and thin, will ride it out with me. And she's just as gorgeous today as she was the day we said "I do."

We all start to eat. Life is truly beautiful.

"Papi, am I allowed to give out our phone number? Mami says I have to ask you."

"To whom?" I ask as I scoop another mouthful onto my fork.

"His name is Carson."

I choke.

Jenna reaches over and smacks my back while laughing.

She's not even a teenager yet. Why do boys want to

call her? She's too beautiful. She looks too much like her mother.

There is no way a boy will be calling my house. Does he know who I am? I'm a motherfucking Hellion. No, he can't call my daughter.

I swallow hard. "No," I answer and drink some sweet tea.

"But, but…" she whines.

"No buts. No boys." I stand firm in my decision.

Suddenly losing my appetite, I pick up my plate and take it to the garbage to clean it off.

My baby girl, my first born, wants to have a boy call her.

I think back to young Jenna: her long, dark hair falling in waves down her back; her innocent laugh at everything Julio or I said or did. Her love for me has remained my constant, my lifeline. Then I think of the hell I put her through.

No way will my daughter have a boy calling this young.

I shake my head as my phone pings with a text from Boomer.

I don't think about anything beyond my daughter, my baby girl wanting to have a boy call her as I walk outside. My daughter wants to have a boy call her? Just another season in life I'm not prepared for.

Boomer pulls up on his Harley, and I'm already in

the backyard opening my shop door while my bearded brother parks before making his way inside.

"Why do you look like someone ran over your dog? You don't even have a damn dog," he jokes.

"Maritza wants to have a boy call her on the phone."

Boomer busts out laughing. "You look like you could puke, and it's all because a little boy wants to call your preteen daughter?"

I shake my head. "You don't have girls; you have boys. Boys are different. You also aren't with a woman who has been in love with you and only you since she was, like, nine."

"Vida's loved you that long?"

I smile proudly. "Mine, all fucking mine."

"Just let the boy call and tell him he has to pass the Hellions' test. He'll take one look at Roundman and pee his pants."

We both laugh. "True." I move to the back of the shop. "Do you just need new brackets to mount the saddle bags or the whole kit?"

"Better do the whole kit if you aren't gonna use it."

I smile, thinking about a road trip on my bike with Vida.

"As nice as the idea is, we have babies, so for now, we stay home. I don't need the bigger bags."

"Pami is used to being ready to run at any moment, even after all this time. I swear the woman packs for a week if we're just going down the road. I've gone across country with my current bags, but she says I need bigger."

"And who says size doesn't matter?" I joke.

We both laugh. Then he gets the kit. It takes a little while, but we eventually get the new saddlebag brackets and bags on his bike.

As he revs his engine and pulls away, I think about my wife inside. By now, my kids should be ready for bed, which means I don't have to think about boys and my daughter. I need to think about giving my wife another son or daughter.

With that, I walk back in my house with a smile on my face and a dick that hardens with each passing moment from just thinking about planting a seed in her womb.

JENNA

Jenna

After dinner, I quickly go through my evening routine with the kids, my anger building as I move through the motions.

I know Maritza and boys are a tough thing for a father to face. I understand his mindset when he had to get up from the table. However, when the sound of the Harley pulling away hit my ears, my temper hit the roof.

He left without saying good-bye. I will put up with a lot of shit, and I mean a lot of shit, but after everything we went through, that is not something I will let slide.

He wants the heat. He wants the fire. Well, it's smoking hot now.

I hear the bike again, and I want to beat him on the head with a frying pan. I go about the task of making muffins for the kids for their lunches next week, and I'm fighting to tamp down my emotions when Ruben walks in happier than when he left.

This only makes me more insanely angry.

"Vida," he greets as he takes off his shoes and strips off the T-shirt he had on for dinner. He tosses it to the floor, and I want to strangle him with it.

"I'm not picking that up, asshole."

He smirks as he walks into the kitchen. "I'll take care of it later. I want to take care of you now."

When he reaches out to put his hands on my hips, I react without thinking. The egg in my hand goes flying right onto his forehead where it cracks, yolk running down his face.

He backs up from me and looks at me like I have completely lost my mind.

Maybe I have.

I grab my kitchen towel and start swinging it at him. "You left, and you didn't speak. You left me and your children, and you didn't say one word. Ruben Castillo, you need to respect me, respect us more than that. This is not a fast food restaurant where you can have it your way."

He laughs as he catches the end of my towel and uses the leverage to jerk me toward him, yolk running down his nose and cheeks. He blinks, and I feel bad when it gets in his eyelashes.

"Ardiente," he whispers.

"Asshole," I whisper back.

"I didn't leave. Boomer needed my old saddlebags and brackets. I met him outside, he pulled up on his bike, we changed them, and *he* pulled off. That's the bike you heard. I have more respect for you and our children than to leave without saying something."

I feel so stupid. I overreacted.

Taking the towel, I wipe the egg off his forehead and eyes as he smiles at me.

"Sorry about my freak out."

"I love it when you give me shit." He brushes his lips against mine. "It shows me you care." Yolk from his face rubs onto my cheek. "Most men would like a quiet, submissive wife. I'm not most men. I married my woman for her fire. Don't ever hold back from me, not ever." When his lips crash down on mine, I am lost in him immediately.

Fire. I feel the heat between us. We have fire.

PASSION BURNS

RUBY

J enna brings her hands up to my face, her thumb resting on the ruby tattoo under my eye. "I have a perfect gem in you," she whispers.

"I'm far from perfect."

"You're perfect for me. You were made for me and me for you."

Leaning down, I kiss her, slowly at first until I begin

to drink her in, our tongues tangling. I can't get enough. She is the air I breathe.

I back her into the corner of our cabinets where, gripping her ass, I scoop her up onto the countertop. She moans yet doesn't stop kissing me.

I reach the hem of her shirt and begin to pull it up, but she tugs it back down.

"My marks," she whispers against my lips, "the lights are on."

My mind stops for a moment. Anger fills me that these men marked my wife for life.

Scooping her up, I wrap her legs around my waist as she holds my neck. I carry her to our bedroom and lay her on our bed.

Lying back, I let her get comfortable then step back to shut and lock our bedroom door.

Tapping the touch lamp on the side of our bed, I have light, but it's not so intimidating with its brightness. It's time my wife gets her body back.

When I go to lift her shirt, she again tries to tug it back down.

"Baby, those marks are life."

Tears fill her eyes.

"Hear me out," I plead as I lie down beside her and trace my hand up her shirt. "Every stretch mark they traced was created by us. Don't let them take that away. They cut them; they cut you. But, baby, you stayed strong for our babies. You lived when most people would have given up and begged for death. Those marks aren't something to hide, but something to be proud of." I kiss her.

She doesn't resist, and when her arms wrap around me, pulling me to her, I know she is out of her head … at least for the moment.

I pull back and slide her shirt up. Then, kissing my way down her body, I spend time giving attention to each stretch mark they touched, begging, "Let me plant my seed, Vida. Let's make new life together. Let me grow your body once again with my baby."

Reaching the waistband of her pajama pants, I slide them down with her panties, leaving her exposed to me. Then I trail kisses up the inside of her legs, alternating sides as I make my way up to her sweet juncture where I part her lips before licking and blowing as she arches her back.

She moans as she grabs my head, wanting more, her legs wrapping around my neck as I fuck her with my tongue then insert two fingers as I suck her clit.

"Please, Ruby," she cries out breathlessly. "Ruben," she whimpers as she spasms, her inner walls gripping my digits through her orgasm before her legs fall open, relaxing, coming down from the aftershocks.

I pull away and nip at her inner thigh. "You are my life, Jenna. Make life with me. I want another baby."

When I look up, she bites her bottom lip, nods her head, and smiles.

I kiss her as I lie over her. "I love you, Jenna Castillo."

"Just remember, I'm not signing shit." We both laugh, having come so far. "I'll be the one and only Mrs. Ruben Castillo."

"For the past, for the present, and for the future, you are the one and only."

I mean every word of it. She is my one and only.

Sometimes, you have to let someone go so you both can work on yourselves to be better for each other. The saying is true: if it's meant to be, it finds a way.

I kiss her until she is pulling at me for more.

Getting up, I slide my sweats and boxers off before climbing back over my wife and lining up, sliding my hard cock into her slick, wet pussy. I groan in pleasure as she wraps her legs around me and thrusts her hips up to meet mine while I rock into her.

"Gonna plant my seed. Gonna make my woman pregnant with my baby."

Jenna laughs. "No baby talk while we're fuckin'."

I laugh. "No, we can talk about making babies, just not about feeding or clothing them. If I had my way, we would make a baby every time I enter you. Our connection is that strong," I say as I slide in and out of her.

"We make beautiful babies," she whispers, tightening as she builds toward her climax.

"They have a beautiful mama from the inside to the out. She's the life to our whole family," I whisper against her lips before kissing her.

I hold myself deep inside her and let her inner walls milk me. Then my spine tingles and my balls tighten. I slide out and back in four more times before I explode inside of her.

We have heat.

EPILOGUE

SIX WEEKS LATER...

Jenna

"Are you sure he's going to get the meaning behind this?" Pam asks me as we leave the garden supply store.

"If you knew just how many times he talks about planting his seed, you would get it." I laugh.

"Look, it took me a while to understand the black picket fence thing with all the Hellions. I don't even want to try to understand proposals, weddings, and pregnancy announcements."

I shrug my shoulders. "We ol' ladies have codes, too. A black picket fence is off limits for a barfly. I'll cut a bitch if she comes in my house and thinks she can touch my man. Proposals, it's about the ride, Pami, always about the ride for life. Pregnancies, I suppose it depends on your man. Mine happens to be like fertilizer: once he says he's going to make a baby, it's like miracle grow to my ovaries."

She laughs as we head home.

We pull into her driveway, and she gives me a serious look.

"Do you think Boomer will miss not being able to plant seeds and watch them grow?"

I squeeze my friend's hand. "I think Boomer planted his seed in your heart, and he loves watching you grow into the strong woman you are becoming. I think he finds his garden to be flourishing in the life you guys have made with Colt and Wesson."

She tilts her head, deep in thought.

"One thing I've learned," I tell her, "is don't over-think. Don't box yourself into what you think your man wants and don't give up on who you are because, from the beginning, that's the woman he fell in love with. Don't ever doubt your place with your man, Pami … ever."

She smiles at me. "He does love me through thick and thin."

"Keep it simple, sister." I wink at her. "One day at a time, ride it out."

We hug, make our way inside her home, and I pick my kids up since her mom watched them while we went shopping.

At home, I laugh to myself as I bring in the bags. I really hope Ruben gets the double meaning.

I'm in the kitchen, making dinner, when Ruben comes home. He makes his way to me and his hands immediately grip my hips and pull me to him. With my back to his front, his head drops, and he nips my neck.

I smile. He can't get enough of me, and I could spend the rest of my life loving this moment day after day after day.

"Well, hello, Ruben."

"Vida," he whispers seductively, sending heat down my neck.

I rock my hips back into him. "I'm going to burn dinner if you don't stop."

He backs away, laughing, and then goes to change.

The kids are all in their rooms, playing, when he finds me a few minutes later and wraps his arms around me from behind again. This feeling never gets old: safe, in the arms of the man who loves me. He could stand here, holding me while I finish cooking, but I have other things for him to handle first.

"Ruben, will you put those bags away for me please?"

He kisses my neck before he turns to the bags I left on the counter, opening the first one and laying out the item.

"A garden trowel?" He opens the second bag. "Gloves?" He opens the third bag and holds up the cushion with a questioning look on his face.

"Tools necessary," I answer, continuing to stir my spaghetti sauce.

"Are we growing vegetables now or weeding out the landscaping?"

I laugh. "I know someone in this family who has been very big on planting seeds lately." I turn to him. "I figure the garden trowel will be necessary to hide your money in the backyard if you want to save any. The gloves are for diaper changing time, and the cushion is because we are getting older, Ruby. And when you're on your knees, talking to my belly for the next nine months, you're gonna need a cushion."

His eyes grow wide when he realizes what I'm saying. "Life?"

I nod my head.

He scoops me up and spins me around. "You give me life. You give me love. We made more life." He kisses me softly. "You are my every breath and every heartbeat. You are my world, my love."

Tears fill my eyes as he sets me on the countertop.

He reaches into the pocket of his sweat pants. "I got this for you and wanted to wait until after dinner, but I can't." He opens the small ring box, and I'm flabbergasted as he pulls out the sparkling, black diamond, eternity band. "I know the road we've been on hasn't always been smooth, so today, I give you this ring to recommit myself to you." He looks into my eyes and heat blazes between us. "I love you, Jenna, for the past, the now, and the forever. I thank you and I cherish you for sticking it out in the good times and the bad. This is a circle that is unending, as is our heated ride in life together."

The End...
Until the next ride...

ABOUT THE AUTHOR

About the Author

USA Today and *Wall Street Journal* bestselling author Chelsea Camaron is a small-town Carolina girl with a big imagination. She's a wife and mom, chasing her dreams. She writes contemporary romance, romantic suspense, and romance thrillers. She loves to write about blue-collar men who have real problems with a fictional twist. From mechanics, bikers, oil riggers, smokejumpers, bar owners, and beyond she loves a strong hero who works hard and plays harder.

Chelsea can be found on social media at:
Facebook: www.facebook.com/authorchelseacamaron
Twitter: @chelseacamaron
Instagram: @chelseacamaron
Website: www.authorchelseacamaron.com
Email chelseacamaron@gmail.com
Join Chelsea's reader group here: http://bit.ly/2BzvTa4

ORIGINALS RIDE
Hellions Ride Book 8

Four men, four families, four originals, one club.

Go back to where it all began so long ago for Roundman, Danza, Frisco, and the late Rocky Fowler. A life choice, a road less traveled, all coming together in the name of brotherhood.

Some found love, some faced loss, and others learned real loyalty. This is the story before the chaos.

This is how the originals ride.

RIDE WITH ME

(Hellions MC and Ravage MC Duel)

Ride With Me - Hellions Ride

DO IT BIG

"Southern bred, southern fed, and Lux, I'll damn sure be southern when I'm dead. Love you, babe, but New York ain't the place to be."

She laughs, and I bite back my instinct to smile. There isn't a more beautiful sound in the world than my woman when she is happy.

"Rex, I didn't say move there. It's called a vacation."

"Woman, I own Crews Transports with Tripp. Don't you know, when you have your own business, you're married to it!"

She flashes her left hand in front of my face, the very hand with my flashy ring on it.

"You could be married to me"—she pauses to meet my gaze—"in New York."

Reaching out, I grab her skirt-covered hips and pull her to me. Her heels are so high she falls off balance and into me, just how I like.

My woman, my deluxe model, and my soon to be wife, Caroline. She is sassy and classy and, when she needs to be, trashy. She makes my dick hard and my hard-ass heart soften. There is nothing I wouldn't give her … including a trip to New York.

"Is that what you want?" I ask, knowing damn well I will lay the world at her designer shoe covered feet.

"I have more than I ever thought I wanted already, Rex." She turns her head away shyly, reminding me just how far we have come.

How did a corporate accountant manager tame me, Mister 'hit it, get it, and go, no repeats'? Hell, she got me in a damn suit before I could even claim her as mine.

If my Fancy Nancy woman wants to get married in Central Park, then I will make it happen.

"Lux, you know how this works. If you want it, you've got it, but baby, you've gotta say it." Leaning down, I kiss her. She opens, and I slip my tongue inside, getting lost in her mouth.

Her hands immediately go to my hair and release it from the usual knot on the back of my head so she can run her fingers through it. The pull only makes my dick harder as I back us up to our couch.

Sliding her skirt up and over her hips, I find her thigh highs and unclip the snaps to her garter belt so she has room to move as I fall back and take her with me, forcing her to straddle me on the way down.

Breaking our kiss, I growl, "I know what I want right now. You want the beast, baby?"

She purrs against my mouth, "Always."

"Take it." I take my hands off her and grip the back of the couch.

She reaches between us and unbuttons my jeans. Then I lift my hips as she slides them off.

Standing back, she unbuttons her top, exposing her lace bra. My deluxe woman teases me as she unzips her skirt and shimmies it down her legs. Unhooking her garter belt from her waist, she then removes it before propping her foot on the edge of the couch between my legs.

Unable to resist, I reach out and run my fingers along the edge of her thigh high before kissing her inner thigh and then putting my mouth against her silk-covered pussy. Using my teeth, I pull at the material and graze her sensitive skin while sliding my hands down her leg, taking her leg coverings off.

She rocks against my face, bringing herself to the edge, her hand on my forehead as she pushes me back against the couch.

"If I want it, I take it, remember?" she taunts me.

Unable to sit still as she removes the other stocking and her panties, I take off my shirt and lean back before she climbs over me. And that's when I slide right into her slick, tight heat.

The sensation of her around my cock has me growing even harder. I grip the back of the couch tightly, trying not to explode like a fifteen-year-old inside a virgin.

She slides up and down as her manicured nails draw patterns over my abs while they flex instinctively. My balls tighten, but I refuse to go off until she's gotten at least one good one ... if not two.

I rock my hips up to match her rhythm as she rides me slowly and steadily. My seductress knows how to play my body like a damn instrument.

Growling, I fight not to lose control and take over, because I love when Caroline takes what she wants from me. There is nothing hotter than a woman who knows how to work me up.

Suddenly, my phone rings with Tripp's ringtone. Dammit, I know I should answer. He's my club president, business partner, but more than that, he's my cousin by blood and raised as my brother. He's also not one to call unless it's business for the club or Crews Transports, and occasionally the call falls into both categories. Either way, he's not one to simply shoot the shit, so I should answer.

Regardless, my woman is on my cock, so the phone can wait.

As I give my attention back to Lux, my phone immediately rings again with Tripp's ringtone.

Damn.

Caroline slides down on my dick and stills. Leaning over, she grabs my phone and hands it to me.

"Brother," I answer as Lux rolls her hips, distracting me, "somebody better be dead or dying. If no one is bleeding, when I find you, someone will be."

Tripp laughs. "Having some quality time with Lux, I see."

"What the fuck do you want?" I growl.

I hear Doll, his ol' lady, laugh in the background.

Caroline drops her head to my neck and bites as I

reach up and roll her nipple rings between my fingers. No way am I going to let her work me over and not let her know she still has my attention.

"Got a nine one oh," Tripp clips out, giving me the code for a Hellions' transport. This isn't personal business; this is club business.

"When do we roll out?"

"How soon can you be ready?"

Lux stills over me, and I see the disappointment in her eyes.

I drop my head back against the couch and blow out a frustrated breath. "How long are we gonna be gone?"

"Undetermined."

Fuck!

"Tripp," I start. "You know I have Axel this weekend."

I absolutely hate letting my ol' lady down, but it kills me to disappoint my son. I missed so much of his early years because I fucked over his mom, Tessie. Therefore, I don't miss any time I get with him now. Thankfully, Tessie and her man Shooter understand my lifestyle. They should since Shooter is a Hellions brother, but they could be assholes about my schedule, and they aren't. No, somehow in all the mess we made between us, Tessie and I found this new way to co-parent together.

Shooter takes good care of my boy, but he's mine,

and he's so fucking amazing I still have to pinch myself to know I had a part in something so good.

"I'll do my best to get us home in time." He pauses. "You know I wouldn't ask if I felt comfortable with anyone else having my back."

Shit, I know this is true.

"Give me two hours so I can at least go and tell Axel bye and make arrangements with Tessie for the change in schedule."

"Done," he says. Then I can hear Doll whisper something before he says, "Make it three. I have a son to get down for a nap and a wife to fuck. See you at the truck then."

I laugh as I disconnect the call.

"Looks like we better hurry," Lux teases.

"Do I ever hurry with you?"

She bites her bottom lip, and I scoop her up, tossing her to her back before laying over her and sliding balls deep back inside her heat.

RIDE WITH ME EXCERPT

Lux

There is no better feeling in the world than being in Rex's arms. Still, after two orgasms and time lying together on the couch, I know I have to get up and let him go.

Slowly, we untangle ourselves and make our way to our bedroom to get changed. I take a quick shower while he packs for his run.

Rex looks at me with hunger in his eyes as I come out of our bathroom to get dressed. "You wanna ride with me to see Axel?"

"Always," I answer, and I will always ride with Drexel 'Rex' Crews.

After everything this man has done for me, there is no time I will ever deny him anything.

Our relationship started out innocent. My life was in shambles when a co-worker tried to make me his whore.

One by one, Drexel Crews and the Hellions MC stepped in to keep me safe and help me face my past as people turned up dead around me. I was in trouble, and he was going to keep me safe for my friend Delilah 'Doll' Crews. It was a simple favor that turned into so much more.

He's everything I never knew I wanted. We come from two different worlds, but I am the woman I am today because of his love.

Once I've put on jeans, boots, and a T-shirt, I braid my brown hair so I am ride ready. My usual attire is business suits and heels.

There is a freedom to the open road with my man in front of me and his steel horse under me. This is not the life I ever would have pictured for myself, yet at the end of every day, it is perfect.

We head out, making the drive to Shooter and Tessie's house.

At their house, Axel is at the front door before we can even reach the porch steps.

Devon Axel Crews is the spitting image of his father. Tessie and Rex had a long-term, on again, off again, crazy relationship that led to nowhere and caused Tessie a lot of pain. When she really needed Rex, he failed her on more than one occasion. This left the door open for Andy 'Shooter' Jenkins to be the man she needed in her and her son's life. Rex never even knew until recently that Axel is his kid, but the truth is out now, and we have all found a way to forgive the sins of the past and have a future together for Axel.

"Hey, little man," Rex greets.

"Why do you always gotta remind me I'm little?" Axel says with a smile as he hugs his father.

Tessie leans against the doorframe, watching her son but not hovering. She is good at giving Axel the space to learn and grow yet still being present. She's a damn good mom, and one day, should I be blessed to have children of my own, I hope I can find the balance she has.

Rex steps up onto the porch and leans in to give Tessie a quick hug while Axel charges in the house like all little kids do. I quickly hug Tessie, as well, and then we all make our way inside.

"I've got a run, Tessie," Rex sighs. I know it kills him to miss a weekend with Axel.

"No worries. You can get him when you get back. Andy and I were going to have date night, but we can reschedule. Mom's not feeling well, so I'm not sure about leaving him with her."

Tessie's mom has multiple sclerosis and suffers daily. Therefore, she's not always the best babysitting option for Axel.

A thought hits me, and I speak before I think.

"Can I have him for the weekend?"

Tessie looks at me wide-eyed while Rex smirks in a way that makes me think he likes the idea of me with his son. I think I may have just overstepped my boundaries with his baby's momma, though.

"I'm sorry. I didn't mean—"

"Are you sure?" Tessie asks, smiling as she reads my face. "I'm good with it if you are, and you can still have him when you get back, Rex. I don't want him to miss time with his dad," she says to him before turning back to me. "Caroline, you are a part of his life, too, and I trust you, just like Rex trusts Andy to keep Axel on his own."

That's all the boost I need, so I nod my head and start planning a weekend with my soon-to-be stepson.

I can do this.

Giving Rex a few minutes with Axel, I feel a tightness in my chest at the thought of him leaving. This isn't the first time he's taken a run since we have been together, and I know it won't be the last. It's just making plans, such as a wedding, is really hard to do when I don't know if he will be home from one day to the next.

"Lux." Axel walks over to me with his dad. "Since it's me and you this weekend, can we have a movie night?"

I smile at him. "Sure thing."

"This way, we can crash out in the living room, and

I'm in a better place to protect you." He looks up to Rex for approval.

"Protect me, huh?"

"Yeah, with Dad having to take a transport for the business and you being alone, someone's got to be the man in the house." He pauses for emphasis and looks me up and down. "Lux, I'm just saying, you are way too much woman to ever be a man."

We all bust out laughing.

"Well, I'm sure your dad is glad to know that."

"Pick up the good popcorn in the pop-up bowl, and I'll be sure to pack the *Transformers* DVD collection from Shooter's stash. If you're lucky, we can squeeze in *Pixels*, too."

With my weekend plans in place, I follow Rex out after a quick good-bye to Tessie and Axel.

I wrap my arms around my man a little tighter in pride that, even while he's gone, not only does he trust me with his son, but Tessie does, too. We really are going to make this blending of our households work. I had such a strange childhood, so I want to make sure Axel doesn't have any doubts about Rex's place in his life.

My mother was the governor's maid by day and his whore by night. I was the bastard child he hid away in the servants' quarters and gave hand-me-downs to from his legitimate daughter. I went to college and had to find a way to pay for it, becoming a whore of my own making to a sugar daddy. I did what my mother did best. I'm not proud of what I did, but in the end, I'm a better person for it.

It's all in the past now, and I have a good man with a good son. I also have a family in the Hellions MC I never thought possible. Life is good, and I really couldn't ask for more.

I start thinking just as Rex drops me off at home. I shouldn't ask for more. Rex has given me so much already. He's right; New York isn't his place. He's a southern boy.

Good-byes are never easy, so after a quick kiss, I make my way inside as he pulls away.

He always tells me, if I want something, take it. Well, I want to be Mrs. Drexel Devon Crews, and I want to do it when he comes home. Now I just need to make it happen.

The ride continues on in Ride with Me (Hellions MC and Ravage MC Duel) co-written with Ryan Michele

ALSO BY CHELSEA CAMARON

Love and Repair Series:

Crash and Burn

Restore My Heart

Salvaged

Full Throttle

Beyond Repair

Stalled

Box Set Available

Hellions Ride Series:

One Ride

Forever Ride

Merciless Ride

Eternal Ride

Innocent Ride

Simple Ride

Heated Ride

Ride with Me (Hellions MC and Ravage MC Duel with Ryan Michele)

Romance – Moments in Time Anthology

Shenanigans (Currently found in the Beer Goggles Anthology

She is …

The following series are co-written

The Fire Inside Series:

(co-written by Theresa Marguerite Hewitt)

Kale

Regulators MC Series:

(co-written by Jessie Lane)

Ice

Hammer

Coal

Summer of Sin Series:

(co-written with Ripp Baker, Daryl Banner, Angelica Chase,
MJ Fields, MX King)

Original Sin

Caldwell Brothers Series:

(co-written by USA Today Bestselling Author MJ Fields)

Hendrix

Morrison

Jagger

Stand Alone Romance:

(co-written with USA Today Bestselling Author MJ Fields)

Visibly Broken

Use Me

Ruthless Rebels MC Series:

(co-written with Ryan Michele)

Shamed

Scorned

Scarred

Schooled

Box Set Available

Power Chain Series:

(co-written with Ryan Michele)

Power Chain FREE eBook

PowerHouse

Power Player

Powerless

OverPowered

CPSIA information can be obtained
at www.ICGtesting.com
Printed in the USA
LVHW051929080321
680888LV00012B/1693